Dax
Copyright 2017 by Nana Malone

This is a work of fiction. Names, characters, places, and incidents either are the product of the author's imagination or are used fictitiously, and any resemblance to actual persons living or dead, business establishments, events, or locales, is entirely coincidental.

Dax

COPYRIGHT © 2017 by Nana Malone

All rights reserved. No part of this book may be used or reproduced in any manner whatsoever without written permission of the author except in the case of brief quotations embodied in critical articles or reviews.

Cover Art by Jena Brignola

Edited by Tanya Saari

Proof Editing Angie Ramey

Published in the United States of America

DAX

NANA MALONE

SANKOFA GIRL

To Naa Ardua for having the courage to go after your dreams.

PROLOGUE

Dax Coulter fidgeted in his seat, loosening his tie as his agent fielded calls. His mother placed a hand on his shoulder, a sign for him to stop and sit still. How the hell did she expect him to be calm? This was his future. And he was about to let everyone down.

His father sat across the room next to his grandfather, who was loudly ranting on and on. The old man was furious, and he wanted everyone to know about it. Dax had to give props to his dad, though; he'd managed to keep Gramps mostly off his back.

Nerves had never been Dax's problem. But it was the third day of the draft, and no one had expected they would still be sitting there. No one except himself, that was. Was it okay that in some weird way he didn't *want* to be drafted?

He rolled his shoulders and tried to relax. He hadn't slept a lot in the last few weeks. This weekend could make or break his career, and the closer it got, the sicker he felt.

He had this recurring nightmare where he went undrafted, and his grandfather forced him to go door-to-door, begging team owners one by one to sign him. Only to have them slam every door in his face.

Who are you kidding? You did this to yourself.

As Gramps had said all along, the Coulter name would only carry Dax so far. His family was the stuff of legends—sports mags, even. And it had always been clear that he didn't measure up.

Rory Coulter, his grandfather, had been magic on the football field and at the Olympics. His grandmother Serina was an Olympic icon. His father a basketball and baseball star. His mother a dancer. And don't even get him started on his siblings. *He* was the bad apple.

The agent hung up the phone and they all quieted down, waiting to hear what news he had.

"Okay, nothing official yet, but what I'm hearing is it's gotten down to Pittsburgh and Dallas. It'll probably be this round. Dallas picks before Pittsburgh, so we should know what they've decided between them, based on what Dallas does." Vic was using his professional, cautiously optimistic voice.

"Well, obviously if Dallas *doesn't* pick him—" Gramps started, but quickly shut up when Grams smacked his arm.

Dax's father asked, "Do we know *what* each team's concerns are? Maybe there's something we can do to help reassure them."

"It doesn't matter what their concerns are. Anything can be fixed," Dax's mother Julia spoke up. "What matters is that he gets signed. And one of them *will* sign you," she said, reassuring Dax with a smile.

Bile rose in his throat and he turned away, unwilling to watch his grandfather roll his eyes one more time. Gramps's disgust was more than apparent with his sneer.

"We know what they want from him and what has them worried, and it's the same answer for both questions," Gramps said. "The name. They want the Coulter name and what it can bring the team. But it's also what they're worried about. He's going to get noticed no matter where he goes, and the team that takes him is going to want him to be noticed for the *right* things. Good luck with that. Dax can put up decent numbers if he really wants to, but he's got to show up first. How many games did he sit out last season? And everyone knows it wasn't because he was injured. Injuries heal. Injuries you can bounce back from, but reputations..."

"Okay then, I think I've had enough." Dax stood abruptly, crossing the hotel room to the minibar, but his twin sister Echo intercepted him.

"Bryce called. He and Tami cut their practice short so they could stream the draft," she said. She raised her voice in an attempt to drown out the sound of their grandfather's constant stream of criticism. "They wanted me to wish you luck."

"Yeah, well, you don't need luck when you've got the Coulter legacy propping you up, right?" Dax muttered. Sure, he covered with humor, but he really wished his big brother was here. They didn't always get along, but Bryce was the only one who'd understand the pressure.

Half an hour later, Dax and his agent were down in the main hall with the other prospects, their agents, and parents. They all watched the teams' representatives crossing to the microphone to announce their selections.

The Dallas representative crossed and announced their pick. Some random guy, not Dax. *Did you really expect it to be?* The large defensive lineman crossed the stage to shake hands with his new team and pose for photos holding a Cowboys jersey up in front of his suit.

"Must be Pittsburgh," his agent leaned over to whisper.

Dax just nodded. If he were honest, he'd been hoping it would be Pittsburgh. Maybe it might shut the old man up if he proved he was good enough. But the other possibility was that they might take him just because of his grandfather's history with the team. Dax had to admit there was a part of him that hoped it would make his grandfather proud to see the Coulter name on the back of a black-and-gold jersey again. The team would undoubtedly promote the connection every chance they got. And let's face it, *that* was what he knew would make Gramps the happiest.

The old man had been increasingly irritable since retiring from Legacy Sports, the family's sports-equipment retail franchise. The great Rory Coulter needed to be seen. To feel relevant. What better way was there for the old man to live vicariously than through the only one of his grandchildren to follow him into football?

The Pittsburgh rep crossed the stage, and Dax wiped his palms on his pants. He closed his eyes and dragged in deep breaths as he listened for his name. *Any* second now...

It didn't come. *Fuck.* He gritted his teeth, but he clapped for the lucky player whose name had been tacked onto the back of the jersey moments before. He recognized the guy, a defensive tackle, from a few match-ups they'd had over their college careers. Dax had evaded the guy's grasp every time they'd gone head-to-head.

During the brief break before the next team took the stage, Dax glanced back toward the area where his family members were sitting. Echo was massaging her temple. No doubt picking up on his stress. His mother's frown deepened. His father patted her knee. They didn't notice him watching them. He was familiar enough with the looks on their faces to know what they meant.

Gramps, however, looked...happy. There was a smug, I-told-you-so smile on his dour face that told Dax everything he needed to know. As far as his grandfather was concerned, the Steelers were *his* team, and Dax didn't make the cut.

He slumped farther into his seat, his eyes pointed at the

stage and his ears blocking out everything that wasn't his own name. He'd fucked up. And now it would cost him everything.

It finally came. In the *fifth* round, the Jacksonville Thrashers announced that they had selected Dax Coulter. His agent nudged him to his feet, and in a daze, Dax made his way to the stage and shook his new boss's hand. He was given a blue jersey with his name emblazoned on a strip and adhered to the back with Velcro. Cameras flashed, and he plastered a smile on his face.

He'd just been drafted by the league's worst team.

ONE

Asha Wix forced herself to sit perfectly still in her seat. There was no way the big brass would take her seriously if she looked like a twitchy kid. *Be poised. Be perfect.* Her father's words rang in her head.

Yeah, but do you even want this job?

Yes, she wanted the job. Well, a job in sports marketing. It didn't matter that football wasn't really her love. It was her brother Damon's love and the only way to get their father's attention. So football was her love by default, as well. And if she could convince these guys, then Jacksonville would officially be her home.

"Miss Wix, your resume is outstanding."

She tilted up her chin. "Thank you. I've had sports marketing internships since I was sixteen."

"For those internships, were you in the promotions arm?"

She knew what he was asking, what the assumption was. That because of her looks, and her age, the only things she knew about sports marketing was how to wear the tiny shorts and low cut tops, and convince drunken revelers to buy swag and alcohol they didn't need. "No. I've always worked in the front office.

Probably the one with the most weight would be when I was assistant to Terry Mansfield with the Ravens the summer I turned eighteen. That's the real meat of my experience."

Terry had been amazing. She'd seen a kindred spirit in Asha. Taught her everything she knew. Number one lesson: Balls of steel. Number two lesson: Never let them see you sweat. Number three lesson: Never, ever, under penalty of losing your feminist card, get involved with anyone in the franchise. Not anyone in the front office, not the players, no one. It would follow her around the rest of her career.

Well, that wasn't hard. She didn't date. Like, ever. Sure, every once in a while she'd go out, but she had a goal, a vision. And sleeping with pompous, knuckleheaded football players didn't fit into that vision.

"I have to tell you, Asha, that the sample marketing plan looks outstanding, and with your connections, you could make a great home here at Jacksonville."

She narrowed her gaze. "My connections?"

"Sure. Your brother just went second round to the Patriots. The great Damon Wix. And of course, there's your father's influence with the owners. You have the connections this franchise is looking for. You'll be a terrific asset."

She pursed her lips. *Breathe, breathe.* She'd been afraid of this. This was not the first franchise to make the same assumptions. Pushing herself to her feet, she closed her binder. "Thank you for taking the time to meet with me, but I am my own person. I'm not bringing my connections with me. Yes, I have my brother, and to some extent my father, but I'm not going to use them to do my job. I am very good at what I do. You either take me alone, or you hire someone else." She held her breath as she walked to the door. She wasn't settling for less than she deserved. Not anymore. As her hand clasped the doorknob, her interviewer spoke up.

"Wait." When Asha paused, he continued. "You're willing to walk away from this job?"

She turned slowly. "I know what I'm worth, and I don't have to settle." Now if only she could say that to her father.

He studied her, nodding slowly. "You, Miss Wix, are exactly what the franchise needs."

She smiled. "I'm glad you see it that way."

"When can you start?"

TWO

"You guys sucked out there!" Coach Moore yelled at everyone in the locker room, as they trickled in from the field. "How many times did we go over that route in practice, huh?" he screamed in Bleday's face. "I know it was at least a hundred! Maybe next time, we make it a thousand! And you!" He leaned into Dax's face now. "Do you need me to coat your hands in glue so you won't drop the ball?"

Dax flushed. He knew he should have had that ball. But he'd looked away to make sure Samuels was still blocking him, and in that fraction of a second, the ball had slipped through his hands. He should have been focused on his job. *Fuck.* But in practice, the guy wasn't fast enough. Dax had been wide open, and would have been able to run it for a touchdown. Instead they'd been forced to punt it away, and that was where their special teams unit had failed. The loss wasn't entirely his fault, but he had contributed to it, and everyone knew it. Shit, as far as *he* was concerned, it *was* his fault.

"I guess it wouldn't hurt if you did," Dax muttered. He should have shut the fuck up, but he was incapable when someone was in his face. He always rose to the occasion. *Dax the Dick, at your service.*

"You think this is funny? Do you?" Moore had been about to move on to the kicker who'd missed three field goals in the second half alone, but instead, he turned back to Dax. "For that, you're in early every day this week, working with the medicine ball until your arms feel like they're going to fall off. If you drop another pass like that during a game, I'm pulling you out!"

Dax rose to his feet and turned away from Coach, pulling his pads off and tossing them into his locker.

"Where do you think you're going?"

"To get a head start on those medicine ball workouts," he called over his shoulder as he grabbed his towel and headed to the showers without being dismissed.

He could hear the Coach fuming and yelling at the rest of his teammates, but he knew it wasn't up to the guy whether or not he was traded to another team. On the other hand, if the rumors he'd heard were true, it was Coach Moore who had to watch out.

Dax relaxed under the hot water of the shower, luxuriating in the fact that he had the room to himself for a change—no one else would dare to storm out on Coach the way he just had.

It would work out all right, though. At least, he hoped. The media were always begging the brass for post-game interviews with him, and the fact that he would be cleaned up first only made it easier for them to get what they wanted...which was what the Powers-That-Be upstairs wanted, too.

He'd been told as much when he was signing his final contracts. They'd chosen him for the name. And while they were pleased with his college performance, they needed someone who would draw fans to the stadium and put asses in the seats. People would show up to watch a Coulter. They'd either see a flash of the remarkable talent he supposedly possessed, or they'd see a flash of something equally entertaining. Dax often wondered if anyone would notice if he had one of his brothers stand in for him. If all they wanted was a Coulter, surely any one of them would do. Right?

Of course there was also the possibility that he might get traded. There were plenty of people hoping he would be. From the coaching staff, to management, to the players. Hell, even his own family was waiting for him to screw up.

He loved them, but he was so tired of hearing, *Bryce this*, and *Bryce that*, the biggest one of all right now being Bryce's upcoming wedding. If Dax had thought Bryce's injury and subsequent rebirth to repeated glory would take some of the pressure off of him, he'd been all wrong.

Meeting Tami while recovering had transformed his brother from the revered oldest son to the epitome of the perfect child, complete with the high achieving, athletic, and talented wife-to-be, whose Cinderella story enchanted the media. Honestly, the whole thing made him want to barf. He liked Tami. A lot, actually. And he was happy his brother could do what he loved again. Hell, all he'd ever wanted was for Bryce to notice him. But perfect child, he was not. And hearing about how perfect Bryce was all the time was a downer.

Once Bryce recovered, Dax was back to being the screwup, the brother whose exploits brought shame to the family's impeccable reputation. A pox on the Coulter clan.

As far as he was concerned, he'd tried repeatedly to live up to his family's expectations—but failed. Every single time. Though to be completely honest, they were his grandfather's expectations—not everyone's.

Bryce had shown an early passion for tennis, which was easier in some ways. But he and his twin sister Echo were more inclined to their grandfather's dual passions: running and football. It was running that Gramps had turned to during the off-season in those early years playing football. And it was running that took him to the Olympics, where he'd met their grandmother.

Echo came out of the womb running, so Dax took up football. He'd shown an aptitude to all sports, but he wanted his family to be proud of him—scratch that, wanted *his grandfather* to be proud—so it was football or nothing.

Echo made him and everyone else proud—she had been running in marathons since she was sixteen, and had finished in the top five in each of the last ten she'd run. She was a shoo-in for representing the US at the next Olympic games, and each year she inched closer to being the first American woman to win the Boston Marathon since the 1980s.

Dax...had been *less* successful. Maybe he'd blown some opportunities. And yes, maybe he was a little spoiled. As teenager, he'd invited the comparisons between himself and his grandfather. He hadn't realized then that doing so, bringing his grandfather back to the spotlight in conjunction with himself, would allow Gramps to criticize every play he made, or worse, missed.

"Everything you do reflects not only on yourself, but on your family, and on *me.*"

Gramps had drilled it into him on the rides to and from high school football games. "People will give you attention because of the Coulter name, but it's up to you to hold on to it once you have it. Don't disappoint them, or they'll forget you and move on to the next big thing. You've got talent, but you need to put in the work."

Dax heard the voices of his teammates as they shuffled into the showers. It seemed that for the time being, Coach Moore's ranting was over. Dax shut the water off and grabbed his towel to dry himself, slipping past his teammates with a series of nods before heading to his locker to finish changing.

He shoved his cell phone into his pocket as he made his way back out of the locker room to face the mass of press that stood between him and his ride back to the hotel.

"Coulter! Coulter! How do you feel about dropping that pass?"

"Do you think scoring that touchdown would have changed the momentum of the game?"

"Would you care to comment on the rumors that you'll be traded?"

"If you do get traded, where would you like to go?"

"What did your family have to say after the game?"

"Did your grandfather watch? Will he come down to see you play some time?"

Dax took a deep breath. He knew better than to say anything real. *Never show yourself. Ever.* It was safer. Game-talk it up. Surface, keep it light. He began throwing brief answers to the reporters, who were forced into near silence in order to hear him.

"Dropping a catch like that obviously sucks. You always want to do your best for the team. Jacksonville is home. I don't know that it would have changed the whole game. Just gonna work harder in practice, and pick it up again next week. I'm sure my family watched the game back home, but you know, everyone's always busy. You'll have to ask Gramps what he thinks himself. Other people tell me where to go and what to do, and I just do my best to do my job," he said, winding down as he reached the promise of sanctuary at the players' passage to their private parking area. "I love football and the city of Jacksonville. As long as I have fun on the field, I'm gonna keep playing. Have a good night, everyone." He flashed his Colgate smile, and was blinded by flashes from the cameras.

On the other side of the door, he paused to let his eyes readjust. His phone vibrated in his pocket. Damn. He had a missed call and a text from his old teammate, Damon. Damon was one of the few people on the planet that Dax called a true friend.

There was a familiar bubble of respect, tinged with slight envy, that arose whenever he thought of Damon. The guy was easily his best friend in the whole world, and Dax missed having his reassuring presence in the locker room and on the field. Damon had been picked up in the second round of the draft by the Patriots. Dax knew that if it had been Damon at the offensive-tackle position during that afternoon's game, he wouldn't have taken his eyes off that ball, and he wouldn't have dropped it.

Samuels was fine at blocking to protect him, but Dax wasn't as sure of him as he had been of Damon. Having Damon there was what made Dax good enough. He just didn't trust anyone else.

He did a quick search to see what time the Patriots' game was so he could calculate when would be a good time to try and call Damon back.

Damon had done more than just guard him on the field. Dax owed him for keeping an eye out for him off the field, too. Dax had been all too willing to enjoy the loud music and boozed up girls in clubs and at parties both on and off campus. The parties they'd managed to find while on the road for away games were some of the wildest imaginable.

Dax wasn't a total moron. He knew better thaen to get trapped. It had been drilled into his head by his grandfather. Hell, it was practically a family mantra. But somehow, he always found a way to get up to some trouble. At least, he hadn't fucked up too badly with the girls. Drinking too much, yes. Missed practices, yes. Unwanted pregnancies, no. *Fuck, no.*

The booze had been more readily available than the girls, and that was where Damon had saved his ass.

A number of hangovers led to Dax missing practices, which

his coaches in turn punished him for by benching him for significant portions of the game. One dangerously close call would have cost him his spot on the team, if it hadn't been for Damon.

It had been during pre-season practices before the start of their sophomore season on the team. Classes hadn't started yet, so there was nothing to worry about except double practices three days a week, and single practices the other two days—in other words, plenty of time for partying and recovering.

There were plenty of guys on the team who were over twenty-one, or had found other ways to acquire the wide variety of booze that flowed freely at the multitude of parties that summer—most of which were held off campus.

The one rule everyone understood and agreed to, was keeping the school's name and the team itself as far from that kind of notoriety as possible. Lots of students lived in the Pittsburgh area during the summer, working summer jobs or internships. So it was never *just* the players or the cheerleaders in attendance. The campus police could be trusted to look the other way most of the time, as students made their way back from the Strip district in the early-morning hours. But local cops were only too happy to set up checkpoints in their efforts to crack down on both underage drinking and driving under the influence.

Dax only remembered bits and pieces of that night.

Dax hadn't *over*indulged, at least not compared to what he normally packed away at one of those parties. He'd had half a dozen beers and a few mysterious shots that included much harder stuff. The combination had turned his stomach more than usual.

He'd figured he hadn't had enough to eat that day, or hadn't hydrated enough during practice. Either way, his head began to pound, and after retching in the bathroom to eliminate some of what was churning in his gut, he'd eventually agreed to hitch a ride from some local girl who'd made it clear she wanted to hook up.

If he was being totally honest, he would say that he hadn't paid any attention to the girl all night. He had no clue how much she'd been drinking.

Damon had taken one look at the pair of them, and pulled off a cock block of epic proportions. He'd insisted on accompanying Dax to the team house on campus. Neither Dax nor the girl had been too happy about the decision. But Damon was six-foot-four and two hundred and fifty pounds of resistance. It was impossible to tell him no.

The girl hadn't even driven three miles before Damon had insisted she pull over and let him drive. She'd started carrying on, but in that calm, Damon voice he'd said, "I'm pretty sure you're drunk, and I don't want to wind up in a ditch somewhere."

She'd been belligerent. "I am *not* drunk. I just pre-gamed with some vodka and cough syrup before going into the party. I just feel a little woozy is all."

Damon had just stared at her. "You're kidding right?"

"Nope, cold medicine is in the glove compartment."

Dax remembered that very clearly, only because he'd been terrified of the way the chick was driving.

When she'd finally stopped the car, only to start screaming at Damon, his friend had calmly helped her out and called Safe Ride for her, assuring her they'd deliver her car to her place. Then he turned to Dax.

"Here," Damon had said, handing him a bottle of cold medicine from the glovebox. "Don't drink too much."

Once Safe Ride came for the girl, Damon had taken over driving. They'd hit the first checkpoint a quarter mile later. By the time the officer came over and they got out of the car, Damon had explained that they had been studying with friends when Dax felt ill. Damon agreed to drive back with him to make sure he got to bed all right. "He's a bit groggy from the medicine," he said, showing the bottle to the officer. "Can't tell if it's just a summer cold or early allergies, but he needs rest before practice tomorrow. We've got a big game coming up in two weeks—first of the season."

The cop had been skeptical. But with no open containers visible in the car, and Dax falling asleep on his feet and smelling mostly of sickeningly sweet, artificial cherry, he'd let them go.

Back in the car and farther up the road, Damon had let out a tense breath. "You're damn lucky that mixed crap you drank had so much grenadine in it, or that wouldn't have worked."

A car with four other players in it was pulled over that same night, and all four were cited for underage drinking. The coach had to bench them for two games each, and they were given disciplinary warnings.

One got caught again, and he was kicked off the team two weeks before Thanksgiving. As for the girl, she was underage. Like way underage. Barely eighteen. Dax shuddered to think about what could have happened.

After that incident, Dax was much more careful about the *where, when,* and *how* of his partying and drinking.

He never took those kinds of risks again.

THREE

Dax sat up. "What do you mean they've backed out of the deal?"

His agent Vic took a beat too long to answer.

"Look, Dax. We knew this might be a problem. It shouldn't surprise you. We still stick to the plan. You with your nose clean, no major scandals, and play your ass off. Plaster that smile on your pretty face, and it'll come."

Yeah, but Griffin Sports Drinks was supposed to be the easy endorsement. And he actually liked the product. It was a healthier option for kids, so he didn't have to feel bad for peddling shit full of sugar. "But dude, I haven't even done anything. I've stayed my ass at home. I've played my best. What the fuck more do they want?" The dread settled in his gut like a kettle bell. He knew what they wanted. They wanted him to be a Coulter. Like the rest of his siblings. Seemingly perfect in every way. And he was...not.

Vic sighed. He'd been Dax's unofficial agent since he'd gone to college. Thanks to NCAA rules, Dax couldn't have an agent, or make any money from football, until he went pro. Vic worked for Legacy, so that helped things along. He was more a family adviser. Until Dax had graduated and gone into the draft. "Look, you need to count on me. Let me do my job. We will get you something. You trust me, right?"

The hell he did. Vic was self-serving, and he wanted that brass ring of a Superbowl champion. And he wanted to line his pockets with Benjamins, and blow the money on three-thousand-a-night hookers. But the guy was a shark, had always been a shark, and his clients reaped the benefits. So Dax trusted him that much. He rubbed at the burning spot in his chest.

Since the draft, he'd had bouts of that burning, hollow sensation right at center mast. Like something was burning a hole inside. It scared the shit out of him. Because he knew that shit wasn't physical. Physically, he was fine. Better than fine. He was in phenomenal shape. No injuries, nothing. But still, that burning.

He'd even cooled it somewhat on the partying. And the women, too—which was a travesty, because a guy had needs.

He loved women, everything about them. The way they smelled and moved and flicked their hair. All women—brunettes, blondes, redheads. God, he fucking loved redheads. But lately, he hadn't been that interested. He just wasn't feeling it.

The idea of dealing with that fawning turf groupie who wanted nothing more than to suck the gridiron right off his dick had somehow lost its appeal in the last few weeks since training camp.

Some of his teammates couldn't believe their misfortune. He was legendary for his partying, and they'd hoped to reap the benefits of his name. *Sorry, boys. I have other shit I need to do.*

"Fine, Vic. I'll sit tight."

"Good. I promise you, this will happen. Now, I'm going to inform the family of the next steps in the plan."

As he hung up with Vic, the burning got worse. That's right, his family. Vic didn't work for him, per se. He worked for Legacy. And his agent was about to run to his grandfather to tell the old man that Dax was such a fuckup that he couldn't hold on to a sure-thing endorsement. *Fantastic*. Dax's day just went from bad to worse.

"I didn't ask you to do that, Damon." Asha paced in front of her closet while she tried to find something to wear that said, *Hey, I'm approachable, but also professional.* So far, all she'd managed to come up with was Ice Queen...cold and stiff,... as usual.

"Asha, chill out. I'm only doing what's best for you."

Her brother might not be able to see her, but she narrowed her gaze and let her voice chill several degrees. "You remember the bigger, meaner version of you? The guy you like to call Dad? You're supposed to be on my side."

"And I am on your side." Her brother mumbled. "I just think it can't hurt to know another person when you're alone in a strange city."

"But I *don't* know Dax Coulter. You know Dax Coulter, and from what you've told me, he's not exactly someone I want to hang around with."

"Oh, come on, he's a good guy. And you're my sister, so he'll look out for you like you're his own. Besides, with Dad knowing Brent and doing business with Legacy, it's good to keep the families tight. C'mon, I worry about you, little sister."

Asha sighed, trying to remind herself that he was doing this out of love, and nothing else. "Damon, I understand, but Dad's been breathing down my neck. You think I don't know he's the reason I didn't get the Baltimore Ravens job? I should have been a shoo-in. I've worked with the franchise before. And I've worked with the VP of Marketing before. But no, dad had to get involved with his demands, and then the position went to another candidate. The only reason I got this job, was because I didn't tell anyone I was applying."

Damon sometimes tried to speak for their father. But Asha knew Damon understood exactly what a pill the old man could be, and thankfully, he didn't say much. "Asha, you know it's better to ignore him."

"Yeah, well, not possible. For years, I've tried to get his attention, to get him to notice me because of *me*. When he finally decides to take notice, it's to make demands for a personal box. Sure, he played football, and Rory Coulter was his mentor, but his Superbowl rings will only take him so far. Thank God, I got a job with the Thrashers." Yeah, her father wanted no part of her team. As far as he was concerned, it wasn't prestigious enough. Fine by her. She could make a name for herself and maybe have someone notice how good she was all on her own for once, not because she was Damon's sister, or Marcus Wix's daughter. She was Asha. She could stand on her own two feet. And she didn't need her brother making any friends for her. This wasn't like high school or college. She was an adult. She'd manage perfectly fine on her own. She hoped.

FOUR

Safely ensconced at home, Dax checked his voicemail before calling Damon back. Yeah, that was a big mistake.

"Dax, it's Gramps. You've got to get yourself straightened out —and I'm not talking about that crap you pulled on the field, either," his grandfather's gravelly voice said with force Then his tone dropped lower and he mumbled about the dropped pass that was going to wind up on the sports networks' cycles of bad plays for the next seven to ten days. "Anyway, what I'm really calling about is these rumors out of Jacksonville. My contacts tell me there's truth to some of them, and I know I've already told you to cool your heels when it comes to your extravagant nights out. I know it's your money you're playing with. And if it really were just the money, that'd be one thing, but you're always playing with more than that, and you should have some respect. If not for your father and I, who have done so much to build the Coulter name, then think about your brothers. Fox and Gage don't need to come up with your shadow over them. If you won't do it for yourself or your father, then just think about doing it for them."

Dax's drink almost spurted from his nose. As if he were

actively trying to do any of it to spite the old man. As if he'd ever done *anything* but try to make him proud. And the very idea of Fox and Gage being embarrassed by *his* behavior was laughable. Fox and his group of friends looked down on football from their hockey haze. As for Gage, he was in high school. The tales of his brother's exploits on top of his family's wealth and reputation would only further cement his status as one of the popular kids, especially since he'd already proven himself a basketball king.

He ignored the rest of his grandfather's message and skipped ahead to the one from Echo. He loved his twin. He really did. There were so many ways in which he felt she was the only one who truly understood him. But they couldn't be more different. It was really amazing that they got along at all, with personalities that were designed to clash. But there was something to be said about those nine months of close quarters.

"Hey, Dax. Ignore whatever it was Gramps called you to say. It's not *entirely* your fault you dropped that ball. Your buddy Samuels let that guy who intercepted the ball last week through, so it was only natural for you to make sure you were properly covered. Anyway...looks like you're doing a decent job of keeping the press interested without giving them much to work with, so keep up your vigilance on that front. It sucks, I know, but it's the best way to dodge rumors. If you hear anything, or need someone to talk to, you know who to call."

Dax couldn't help but smile at Echo's efforts to make him feel better. He checked the last voicemail, expecting it to be from his father.

It was from Bryce, though, and after a quick compliment on how great Dax had played, despite the loss and the missed catch, Bryce moved on to asking Dax if he would be best man at his wedding in November.

Dax had already double-checked the Thrashers' schedule,

and so long as he was able to keep himself from getting traded, the wedding was the same weekend as the Thrashers' bye week.

"Please, Dax," Bryce's voice begged from the recording. "And if you do say yes, just remember to keep any plans for the bachelor party tame...ish. Thanks again. We'll talk soon."

Dax shook his head as he turned back to the television where the Patriots' game was winding down. They'd passed the two-minute warning, and the Pats had the ball and the lead. All they had to do was kneel it twice to run the clock out.

Why would Bryce ask him to be best man? Fox managed to keep all his altercations and hijinks limited to the ice as he worked his way up from a minor league hockey team to the majors. But he'd never been one to get too involved in family anything. He usually only attended functions if he was dragged to them. And even then, he always kept to himself.

And Gage, well he was the baby of the family. He and Dax hadn't spent as much time together growing up. They rarely played or even hung out with each other.

To be honest, Dax was a little surprised Bryce hadn't asked Echo to be his best man. The two of them were so close. Then Dax realized that Echo was probably going to be one of Tami's bridesmaids. So, process of elimination, of course. He automatically stuffed down the slash of hurt.

A bright-red, breaking-news ticker at the bottom of the screen caught his attention. The game had ended, and the commentators were back in studio. They were running through the highlights of the day's completed games, along with fantasy football statistics. Dax turned up the volume as the suited men switched their attention to the news that had just come in.

"We have word that ownership over at the Thrashers is drastically shaking things up," said one of the talking heads.

"I'm surprised they're making an announcement like this

today," one of his co-anchors admitted, shock clear in his tone. "Usually, they save this kind of thing until Monday morning."

"I guess they want to send a clear message that they're moving on from not just the last two games, but the last several disappointing seasons."

"Still, to let almost the entire coaching staff go only hours after that kind of loss... While it *does* send a message, I'm just not sure that it's the message they *should* be sending."

"I have to agree with you there." A third man jumped into the conversation. "There is a right way of making this kind of announcement, and there's a wrong way. By announcing it before the day's games are over, it just feels like they're trying to cause the greatest stir possible."

"I think you're absolutely right about that, but I don't know that I agree that's a bad thing."

Dax muted the television again. Coach Moore was out. Dax wondered who else on the coaching staff would be gone. He pulled up his email and news feeds on his phone, but so far there was nothing. It would take a few minutes longer for already-busy sports writers to ferret out the details and write them up. He did locate the press release, but it made no mention of player trades. In fact, the owners seemed to go out of their way to inform everyone that the changes were being made to staffing; the coaching staff and staff in the Thrashers' main offices. Whatever that meant.

His phone rang in his hand. *Damon.* "Hey, man!"

"Dax? Hey, it's Damon." There was a levity in Damon's voice that Dax recognized. It came from playing a good game and knowing it.

"Hey, I was waiting for a good time to call, but wasn't sure when you'd be done. Great game today."

"Thanks. And yeah, I'm guessing there wouldn't be a good

time to call from your end. Just saw the news, man. It's gonna be rough out your way for a while. I do not envy you."

"Tell me about it. I just saw the news myself. But hey, so long as I'm staying put, I'll just roll with things the way I always do," he assured his friend.

"Actually, I guess this shakeup thing is kind of why I called you in the first place. D'you remember me talkin' about my little sister, Asha?"

Asha. He remembered her name, but her face eluded him. His recall buttons were searching for someone that looked like Damon. Huge eyes, dark features, and olive skin, thanks to their Persian mother.

"Didn't I meet her at the draft?"

"What? No, that was my cousin. No, Asha couldn't make it 'cause she was busy studying for finals and working at her internship," Damon clarified.

That was right. Asha was the bookish one. Skipped some grades or something. They'd never met. "Okay, yeah, now that you mention it, I do think I remember you talkin' about her. Why? What's up?"

"Well, she just got a job out your way. Thrashers marketing department or something. I was gonna give you guys each other's numbers so you could get together or something. It'd be nice to know she's got someone there who's looking out for her, you know? Plus, she might need someone there who she can trust, who she sort-of knows."

"But...I *don't* know her," Dax pointed out.

"Naw, but I trust you, and if *I* trust you, she will. I've told you about her, I've told her about you, so it's like you *know* each other. And you can make sure the other guys stay in line, you know what I mean?" Damon rambled. "Look, I've already told her she should look you up. Just wanted to let you know."

What the hell was he going to talk to female Damon about?

Football, probably. "Yeah, okay. I'll let her know that if she needs anything, all she has to do is ask."

"That's all I'm looking for. Thank you." Dax could hear the relieved smile in his friend's voice. "I'll hit you up when we're in Miami. I got a bye week after that, so we can chill."

"You're on." Dax agreed before hanging up. It would be good to bring a piece of his old life to Jacksonville. Even if it was only by association.

He turned the volume back up on the TV, and left the channel on one of the local sportscasts.

How *had* Damon's little sister managed to land a job like that so soon after graduating? For that matter, how old could she be? Damon was about the same age as himself, and they'd both only just graduated. How *little* could his little sister possibly be? *Not your concern.* Because no matter what, the girl was off limits. He pictured Damon disemboweling him for even looking at his sister sideways. Oh yeah, that threw a cold shower on any wayward thoughts. Besides, he had too much shit to deal with to navigate that kind of minefield.

FIVE

Asha self-consciously brushed the hair out of her eyes, tucking it behind her ear, as she pulled her shoulders back and with as much confidence as she could muster, strode through the doors at Thrashers headquarters.

The frantic energy in the building was palpable as she headed for the elevators. Even the janitorial staff was watching everything and everyone as they went about changing the bags in the trash bins, looking over their shoulders for someone who might be watching them. A haggard-looking security guard was gulping coffee.

Asha and the other new hires had been advised to arrive at eleven o'clock. Supposedly, to give those employees who were being let go a chance to clear their old workspaces before their replacements arrived.

She hadn't run into anyone leaving as she came in, but looking at her watch, she was a bit early. It was only ten forty-five. Asha had never felt that showing up exactly on time was good enough. It was better to show up a few minutes early, to show her enthusiasm and commitment to the task at hand. *Way to dork it up on your first day. Good way to make friends.*

Pushing the button on the elevator, Asha forced the thought out of her head. She refused to psych herself out about it. She was used to having people...well, not *hate* her exactly. But somehow, she'd always managed to step on a few toes as she pushed ahead in school, taking over at the top of the class and holding firm once she got there.

Today was looking like it was going to be very interesting.

Raised voices caught her attention when she stepped off the elevator. She did her best to ignore them, and made her way down the hall. The conversation she'd had with her new boss during her interview trickled back into her head.

"We've made trades over the years. Signed fresh blood and shifted players around for our salary cap—even when we haven't had major injuries, we've had abysmal records the last few seasons. It's not a simple matter of changing up the players. Bigger changes are needed—*radical* and unexpected and thorough changes are needed," he had warned her.

She assured him she was game for anything; that she had not only the necessary knowledge of the sport, but the industry, and of being the odd woman out, as well.

"I'm used to difficult situations," she'd said. "I thrive on them."

But, she admitted to herself, thriving on them and enjoying them were two different things. She continued down the corridor to the right, where she'd been told the staff offices and cubicles were located. Before she wandered too far on her own, a short, plump woman in a turquoise pantsuit appeared with a tablet computer and a grin.

"I'm Linda, and you must be Ms. Wix," the woman greeted her with a handshake. "I'm the receptionist around here. Though, today I feel more like a referee. I'll show you to your new workspace and to the break room. There's a meeting in forty-five minutes where you'll hear the plan for your department moving forward, and will get your assignment."

"Pleased to meet you, Linda. And please, call me Asha, or Ash, either works," she babbled, falling a few steps behind. A flash of pity filled her, as she spotted a stony-faced, middle-aged man leaving the offices, carrying a cardboard box of his belongings with as much dignity as he could muster.

"It'll probably wind up being Wix," Linda said with a smile, bringing Asha's attention back. "That okay?"

"Sure. I might look over my shoulder for my brother the first few times, but I'll adjust," Asha said with a laugh.

"Hold on to that attitude," Linda advised. "It's gonna be a rough week all around. This is your cubicle. Conference room is over there," she pointed. "And there's coffee in the break room through here. I'll leave you to get settled in. Oh, here," she handed Asha a sticky note with several words scrawled across it. "Your logins and passwords. They're all temporary, so once you get yourself squared away, be sure to change them. And welcome aboard."

Linda gave Asha a nod and a grin before heading back toward the elevator, chatting sympathetically with her departing colleagues on her way to greet the new recruits.

Asha flopped into the chair, then promptly spent the next ten minutes on her knees, her heels conveniently tossed into a corner by an empty filing cabinet, while she adjusted the height and support.

Behind her somewhere, someone whistled, followed by a couple of more descriptive comments made in appreciation of her assets. *Asshats.* Just what she wanted in the first half hour of her new job. She was less than surprised, though. She was used to the attention. And unfortunately, she'd had to become an expert at deflection.

After a few minutes, her phone alerted her to the meeting.

She plastered on a smile and introduced herself repeatedly as she moved through the quickly-filling room. A quick scan confirmed what she'd already suspected. Most of her colleagues were men. And many of them were also a decade or two older than she was.

There were a few who looked to be about her age. But the only three women she spotted had already found each other and glued themselves together. They looked at her like they wanted to include her, but something seemed to change their minds. Several of her male colleagues were slyly checking her out, and Asha barely refrained from rolling her eyes. She could handle them. She met one man's eyes as she caught him staring and unblinkingly held his gaze. Eventually, he coughed and looked away, his face turning red. Over the years, she'd perfected a series of resting-bitch faces. This was her RBF #3. She refused to be intimidated by anyone.

"Okay everyone, welcome," a middle-aged man said loudly, as everyone found seats. "I believe all of you met with me during the interview process over the last few weeks, but in case somehow you've forgotten, I'm Mr. Adams. Now I want to get right down to business. Moving forward, we're reevaluating how our department interacts with the players so that we can get a better sense of their personalities, and how we can use them to best promote themselves and the team as a whole. We want to get the angles on them that will appeal to our fan base and bring them back into the stadium on Sundays."

He looked around the room and was met with nods of agreement before continuing.

"When it comes to settling in and the day-to-day workings, I want all of you who're new hires to *ask questions*. If you don't know something, don't go trying to look smart and act like you know everything. *Ask someone*. If you have an idea, I want you to share it. What I *don't* want, is for this place to get stagnant again. Those of you we've kept, we chose to keep you for many reasons: loyalty, ingenuity, experience, but mostly, the relationships you have with our players. New hires, that's where we're going to start all of you off—getting to know the players as individuals. I'm going to pair each of you with one of our rookies, and after a few weeks, you're going to pitch at least three ways we can formally introduce these guys to our fans. Veteran staff, you're going to cultivate the relationships you have with the veteran players. See if you can think of new angles. Depending on how things go, we may shake it up a bit in a few weeks and swap the players and members of this team around a bit—give you newbies a few more players to handle once you're settled."

Asha shifted in her seat, curious as to whom she might be paired with.

"Now...what do I mean by pairing you up? Well, you're going to meet with your player for at least fifteen minutes, before *and after* every practice, and every game. You are going to be sitting beside them on the plane, train, or automobile when the team travels. You are going to know their wife's name, their girlfriend, their kids, their mother, father, brother, second cousin once removed. You are going to get them to tell you their deepest, darkest secrets, as well as their hopes and dreams. I want you to know *everything* about them, so that *we* know everything about them. It is through knowing our players better that we become a better team, and that we can *market* that team in the best ways possible."

Mr. Adams moved to a whiteboard, picked up a dry-erase marker, and began writing down pairs of names.

"Mr. Hughes, I want you working with Johnson. Oh, Valazquez, make sure you get them the contact and meeting information. Ms. Wix, you're with Coulter."

What? As in Dax? She raised her hand.

"Excuse me, sir?" she asked, hoping it was just a mistake. She did *not* want to get paired with her brother's old teammate. It wasn't that she had anything against the guy, having never met him, but she had hoped they'd pair her with someone a little more...serious? From everything she'd seen of Dax, he was a bit of a playboy who had more attention for pretty girls than his coaches' instructions, and little to no respect for anything or anyone other than himself. There was also the fact that Damon had gone and given Dax her number and information without consulting her first.

"I said you're with Coulter. Is that a problem?" The challenge was clear from Mr. Adams' tone. It wasn't impossible that they'd done this on purpose. Either to get rid of Dax, or get rid of her.

"You probably know that my brother and Dax Coulter were on the same team in college," Asha said with an understanding smile. "But *I* have never actually met him. If you were under the impression that—"

"We wanted to give Coulter to you *in part* because of his familiarity to your brother, yes," Mr. Adams interrupted. "Coulter is a...tricky rookie to handle. We can only hope your connection to someone he trusts helps him trust and listen to you. *Aside* from that, I was under the impression that you were up for anything. That you were one of the most promising of our new hires. But if you don't think you can handle this—"

Asha grit her teeth. *Challenge accepted.* "I assure you, I can handle Dax Coulter. I just wanted to be sure you we're clear that there is no pre-existing connection between him and me."

"If you haven't met Coulter in person before, you're about to," Mr. Adams said as he handed over the information she would need for her assignment to Dax. "He should have arrived for his pre-practice work-out fifteen minutes ago. He usually runs late, but with Coach Moore gone, he might have gotten curious enough to show up on time. The gym's down near the locker rooms."

Through the rest of the meeting, Asha fidgeted. It seemed the more she tried to get away from it, the more she was stuck with the Wix legacy. But that didn't matter now. If they wanted her to get to know Dax Coulter, then she would get to know Dax Coulter.

At the end of the meeting, she took the information and forced a smile, before turning on her heel and exiting the conference room. She had work to do.

SIX

Asha found Dax in the gym, just where Adams said he would be. He appeared to have just started his workout. He was jogging on a treadmill, wearing headphones connected to an mp3 player that sat in one of the machine's two cup holders.

She stopped to take a long, lingering look. Okay, so she wasn't entirely immune. Well, she wasn't dead, was she? Dax Coulter might look good on the TV screen, but in person he was definitely something to look at. She took her time watching him as he ran, seemingly unaware of her presence.

He was every bit the playboy the media portrayed him as. Tall and muscled, but not as bulky as most football players. Certainly not as big as her brother, at least. She knew part of that was his position. Wide receivers weren't like line backers or defensive tackles, their bodies were not meant to serve as an obstacle to others.

No. Wide receivers needed a degree of maneuverability for evading tackles, jumping higher than the men trying to block them, and above all, the dexterity to catch a difficult throw. She'd seen Dax's numbers from the first two games, and knew his college numbers almost as well as she knew Damon's.

Dax had the potential to post some record-breaking numbers when paired with the right guys, *if* he was willing to put in the work. But he was a wild card. When he was on, he was *really, really* on. When he was off... Well, it was a disaster. A drunken train wreck waiting to happen.

She continued to study him. He wore a loose muscle shirt, and shorts made from a similar breathable material. He'd probably been running for ten or fifteen minutes now, but hadn't really started to break a sweat.

Asha took in his dark hair. It was long enough to have a slight wave but not so long it touched his collar. If he were running a little faster, the muscles in his arms and legs would stand out more prominently.

She'd seen enough pictures of him in uniform on the field and on the covers of tabloids to know that he was pretty. *So damn pretty.*

A prominent jaw, vibrant blue eyes, and straight, white teeth that shone when he smiled completed the face to die for. Oh, he looked good, all right...*and* he knew it. Between his looks and his money, Asha could understand *how* a guy like Dax Coulter appealed to so many women. But it was much more difficult to see what it was about Dax that appealed to her brother so much.

Damon loved Dax like he was his own brother. And Asha knew that Damon wouldn't stick by Dax so firmly if there weren't more to him than what the tabloids said to sell copies. She just needed to see it, too.

She needed to see if she could find the Dax that Damon insisted was there, and then decide whether that Dax was marketable as the black sheep of a sports dynasty.

She took a deep breath, and purposefully strode forward.

She knew Dax had caught her in his periphery, when he startled. He reacted quickly and turned off the machine, grabbing a towel to wipe away the barely-there sheen of sweat from his forehead. Asha had to motion for him to take the headphones from his ears.

"Sorry about that," he said. "Hope you weren't waiting too long to get my attention. I'm afraid I can zone out pretty quickly when it comes to workouts." His eyes were going to kill her—those intent, clear-blue irises. It made her skin tingle.

"No worries. I'm Asha, your new PR rep. I just came down from my meeting upstairs," she explained. "I was told you'd be expecting me, but I don't want to interrupt your workout. I just wanted to introduce myself, and then we can schedule a time—when you're through with practice—to go over—"

"You're taller than I thought you'd be," Dax interrupted. "Damon's always calling you his little sister, so I just assumed... littler." He grinned. "Also more Damon-looking." His gaze swept over her. "Besides your coloring, you look nothing like him." He frowned, as though that fact displeased him.

A flush rose and settled in her face. Asha hoped she wasn't going as red as she feared. Was he checking her out? *Easy does it. Keep your cool. Handle him.* She was the one in charge of this situation. She was the one whose marketing strategy would help determine not only her fate with the organization, but Dax's as well. She was in charge, dammit.

"I need to go over how this is going to work with you. I'd like to accommodate you if I can, but if you're too full of yourself to acknowledge the courtesy of that, then you *will* follow the schedule I set down for you, is that understood?"

His brows shot up, but then he grinned.

"Where'd you get your degree from?" Dax asked, ignoring her statement completely. "I mean, Damon and I *just* graduated, but he's always calling you his little sister. I know you can't be twins, because he'd have told me that," he rambled. His eyes never left hers.

She ground her teeth. "Okay, fine. We'll do it this way, then. Public Relations underwent a large overhaul. The team is changing its approach to just about everything—the coaching style, management, interaction with players, and how we're marketing the team. The first step of the new process is getting to know our players better. To do that, players and members of the marketing team are being buddied up with one another so we can get to know you better, so we can help the *fans* get to know you better," Asha started speaking more quickly to avoid interruption. "I've been buddied with you, so we will be having meetings to chat and develop a plan for how to make *you* more palatable to fans. Our goal is to get butts in the seats out there, and to do that, you guys either need to start winning, or we need to get people to want to see you in person without winning."

She paused to take a breath, and Dax jumped in. "Are you sure you didn't go to school to become an auctioneer? Based on that demonstration, I think you'd be really good at it."

Asha glowered at him. There was a gleam in his eye. She could tell he was enjoying the fact that it bothered her when he completely disregarded what she said. It was unlikely that her complaints would get her reassigned to another player. But that didn't matter, because she had a goal. And she was not giving up just because he made her hot and itchy. She could do this.

"I'd think you'd be interested in hearing what I had to say about a new approach to your image. But if you really are as shallow, parasitic, and lazy as you come off, then maybe it would be better to let my bosses know now so you can save them, and me, the trouble." She inhaled quickly and continued before she lost her nerve. "We don't have to alter a thing, so long as you're content with people lining up to see you crash and burn. It's a bit cliché, but you know clichés only exist because there's a truth to them."

He was still smiling, but she could tell it was no longer genuine. The light in his eyes had dulled. And for a moment, Asha felt a twinge of mingled guilt and regret. She shoved it aside, telling herself that as a football player, there was no way that what she'd just said was the worst thing Dax had ever heard about himself.

Coaches were not above saying anything to rile players into performing. Hell, it was part of how her parents had motivated her to achieve academically, and look at where it had gotten her. Dax would get over it. He could sack up. *If* he even *had* feelings. And if he didn't get over it, he'd undoubtedly complain to her bosses, and they'd reassign her to another player... Or fire her. *Shit*. No, they wouldn't fire her. They had told her how difficult Dax would be. How else had they expected her to handle him? She was all about the carrot and stick. Well, mostly the stick, actually. Screw the carrot.

There was a long pause in the conversation before Dax asked, "So, what've you been up to since moving here? I'm sure Damon will ask me about you next time I talk to him, so you might as well give me something to tell him. We need to pretend to be friendly for his sake. Oh, if you ever need a recommendation for where to go on a night out, you *know* I'm the best person to ask. Though you seem like too much of a killjoy for that."

Killjoy? *Asshole*. "So you're determined to do this the hard way? Ok. If that's all, I think we're done here. I'll go report back to my boss, and I'll be in touch if there's anything further I need from you. Either that, or I'll be fired, or you'll be traded." she muttered. God, he couldn't see her sweat patches, could he? She hadn't realized just how hot it would be in here, and now she was in a hell of a hurry to escape before her skirt and blouse became permanently stuck to her skin. Or she burst into flames. Either one.

"Running off so soon? Too bad. I'll see you around, Asha," Dax called as she left. She grit her teeth as she marched away. He was an ass. A sexy ass, but an ass just the same.

She's off limits, she's off limits, Dax repeated to himself, as he moved from the treadmill to the weight station. Asha Wix was walking, talking sex appeal. *She's Damon's little sister*. If he cared about that at all beyond the fact that it would be a total betrayal of their friendship to hit on Asha. Even worse, Dax was pretty sure he'd never met a woman who was *less* interested in him. And why did that shit turn him on? All women *looked*. He was used to it. Took it for granted even. But not her. As Dax continued his workout, he tried to force his thoughts to a more realistic path—Jen. She was the daughter of two of his parents' closest friends, and had grown up with him and Echo. And she genuinely liked him. She was the kind of girl his grandfather would be happy about welcoming into the family. Not the angry spitfire that had just walked out.

There had been a general push in the family to pair Jen up with Brycebefore he'd met Tami. But it was Dax who'd had a massive crush on her for years. Though, he hadn't really tried too hard to get her to go out with him.

Because the thing was, the moment he did, it would mean settling down. And at twenty-three, that was not happening. The fact that everyone else in the family rejected the idea outright was...disappointing. But it only made him dig his heels in more. They didn't think he was good enough.

Even as his brain tried for an endorphin hit and tried to call up Jen in his memory, it was Asha he saw. Tan, smooth skin. Waves of jet black hair.

And those chocolate-brown eyes. *Shit.* She was beautiful, if maybe wound a little tight. Okay, a lot uptight.

No. No. No. He recognized the signs. The challenge thrown. She was not on the menu. Maybe it would be a good night to head out on the town. There were probably a few guys on the team who would be willing to hit a club or two and celebrate the changing of the guard, as far as the coaching staff went.

There was a lot of pussy running around. But at the end of the season, he *would* make that effort to settle down. He knew his family would be looking for him to do just that after Bryce and Tami's wedding was over. He might as well get ahead of them on that front. Plus, Jen would be a great date for the wedding.

Maybe a better idea would be to get a new rep assigned. Problem solved. Except, she'd know why. And he'd promised Damon to look out for her.

"Hey, Dax," Paul Johnson said as he came into the gym and headed for one of the stationary bikes.

"Yo. Have you heard about our new babysitters? The PR guys are pairing us up with some of their staff to market us better," Dax said, taking advantage of the excuse to pause in his workout. "I think mine's just gone upstairs to try and swap me for someone else."

Paul laughed. "The one in the skirt I passed on my way in here? I'd hold on to her if I were you. Met mine for coffee on the way in. Must've asked me two dozen questions before I finished my cup. Felt like an interview," Paul joked. "Mine wasn't a looker like yours, either. You know, it'll take her a while to get upstairs with those shoes of hers. You can probably make a call in the meantime and get them to let you keep her. Lord knows, I'd take a trade if you don't."

Dax laughed as Paul settled into his workout routine, but he eyed his phone. It was exactly the kind of thing she'd expect him to do. Use whatever influence he had to get his way. She already wasn't his biggest fan. She would expect him to flex his Coulter muscles. She didn't know just how limiting that superpower was. The things he really wanted weren't things he had any control over.

Part of him was inclined to call upstairs and do as Paul suggested. Not for the reasons he suggested, but because of the promise he'd made to Damon. No. Asha would probably like that motive even *less* than if he did it for purely selfish reasons.

No. He'd let the chips fall where they may. He sure as hell didn't need the distraction. *She's off limits*, he began repeating to himself once more. *She's off limits*. Now all he had to do was tell his dick that.

ASHA KNEW SHE WAS TAKING A LONG SHOT WHEN SHE walked to Adams' office.

He looked up from his monitor. "Problem, Wix?"

"Uh, having met with Mr. Coulter—" she began, but was cut off by her boss.

"There will be no reassignments, Ms. Wix. If you do not like your assignment, your options are to shut up about it and do your job or quit. Do I make myself clear?"

She bristled. She'd been called a lot of things—like brown-noser, suck-up, and whiner—by so many of her peers over the years. She'd always been able to tell herself it was jealousy on their part. That it stemmed from their own feelings of inadequacy. The echoes of those labels rang at the edges of her consciousness.

"I was just going to say..." She thought fast on her feet. "That having met with Mr. Coulter, I think you were right to assign him to me. He needs someone who isn't willing to put up with his bullshit, and I won't. I thought I should warn you that *he* might try to call you to have me removed. That *he* might seek a reassignment."

"Oh, I see," Adams frowned, but nodded. "Well, if he does, I'll be sure to tell him the same thing I just told you. There will be no swapping. It's already two weeks into the season. We're behind schedule as it is. Unless there is a legitimate concern with him. Was he inappropriate?"

"No, of course not." Besides his eyes drinking her in. "Let me get out of your hair. I should work on getting better acquainted with the system, and then I thought I'd watch practice from the sidelines."

"Sounds like a plan." Adams turned back to what he'd been working on before she interrupted him, and Asha slunk away to begin the task of reassembling the shreds of her dignity. She'd have to find a way to deal with Dax. And quickly.

She was stuck with him, so she had to make the best of it. Lord only knew she'd been in more uncomfortable situations over the years. Some particularly heinous group projects in college came to mind. It had sucked being younger than everyone else with no way to connect socially. Not to mention the mutters of "jail bait" when she walked through the quad. At least Dax hadn't hit on her. Not outright, anyway. Looks, she could handle. It was the insinuation that breasts somehow negated having a brain that really pissed her off. Like the two were mutually exclusive.

Asha remembered one of her teachers who had suggested she look into marketing at some cosmetics company, or somewhere in the world of fashion. He'd suggested that sports marketing would be difficult if she wasn't willing to use her looks to get ahead. Just how he had wanted her to use her looks remained a mystery.

At least with Dax, she had the buffer of Damon, so he couldn't act like too much of an ass. Not that she'd ever ask Damon to step in. She could handle herself. But Dax Coulter didn't need to know that.

SEVEN

Problem number one: Asha Wix was attractive. Like really, fucking, smoking-hot attractive. *Not* that he was going to do anything about it. Problem number two: she had a massive stick up her gorgeous ass. Like shoved way up there. If she wanted something shoved up her ass, he could think of a slew of other things to shove up there. But he wasn't going to go there.

She even sat stiff as a board while she watched practice. Like she needed a good lay...from someone *other* than him.

She was waiting for him outside the locker room following practice.

"Hello," she said quickly, catching him off guard and startling him. "I just wanted to apologize for earlier. If I came off as rude or...well, anyway. We're going to need to work together for a while, so I figured it would be a good idea if we could just... start again."

Start again? So she wasn't quitting? Well, all right then. Challenge accepted. He grinned at her. "Okay. So how do you propose we go about that?"

She narrowed her gaze, but kept that gorgeous smile on her face. "If there's a time this week that works for you, we could meet to discuss your public image and areas where it can be... improved...for the good of the team."

Dax suppressed a snort. "If you say so. How about dinner tonight? You're new in town, and I can show you a few places. And then we can both let Damon know I checked up on you."

He could tell by her pursed lips she was thinking about declining. But then she said, "Right. I get off work at five. Why don't you meet me downstairs?"

Dax shook his head. "Why don't you give me your address, and I'll pick you up at seven? That should give you time to get home and change."

She eyed him warily. "Text me the info for where you want to go, and I'll dress accordingly and meet you there."

He worked to hold back a smirk. Man, she was stubborn. Hell, she should have been his agent, she was that good at negotiating. "I guess that'll work. I'll see you at seven-thirty then, give you extra time to find the place." He brushed past her, then winked. "I look forward to seeing you tonight, Asha." He said, goading her.

Problem three: he kind of liked it, the back and forth, the fighting with her.

Too many problems, and not enough good solutions.

DAX COULTER PULLED AT EVERY SINGLE COMPETITIVE, irritated nerve Asha had. He was arrogant. Pompous. An ass. He was also a walking pheromone. She was having a hell of a hard time ignoring him. He used his appeal like an axe, with all those winks and the smiles. Damn his smiles and his cleft chin. Well, two could play that game.

It didn't surprise her when the address he sent her turned out to be for one of Jacksonville's hottest clubs. What did surprise her, however, was how good it felt to dress up for the occasion. She'd chosen a simple, form-fitting dress for the night out. Nothing she was falling out of, or that she would be embarrassed to be seen in by her other coworkers, except that there was no hiding her breasts. The fuchsia hue of the fabric, along with the darker eye makeup flattered her dark coloring. Dressing up like this, she looked like her mother. She'd even added a simple henna pattern to her hands as a nod to her heritage. Maybe it was a bit much, but she thought she looked pretty. Not that she wanted to look pretty for Dax Coulter. Oh the lies she told herself.

The look had the desired effect. When she walked up to him at the front of the club, Dax did a double take and stared. "Jesus Christ, Asha."

She bit back the satisfied smirk. "Just one thing, how am I going to get in? I'm not twenty-one yet."

He blinked. "You're not twenty-one?"

She shook her head. "This May."

"It's fine, you're with me. No one will card you." And he was right, they walked right in. The perks of being with Dax Coulter.

Forcing herself to control her smile, she added, "I'd like to say I was surprised you'd pick a place like this, but I'd be lying." She had to practically scream to be heard over the pounding of the bass, as he led them through the club.

Dax waved an arm toward a restricted area off to one side, urging her ahead of him. As soon as they were behind the Plexiglas barrier, the pounding of the music subsided significantly, but the glass still gave them an unobstructed view of people gyrating out on the dance floor.

"It's early in the week," Dax explained. "It can still get pretty busy, but nothing like the weekend. It takes twenty minutes to cross to the bar on Thursday or Friday night."

The passageway they followed opened to a small VIP area with tables and a handful of waiters. The VIP room offered more than just drinks and the handful of food options the club's main bar did.

"Oh," Asha said, as a small menu was placed in front of her. "I ate before I came," she told Dax. "Didn't want to worry about working on an empty stomach."

His lips twitched. "Of course you did," he muttered as he ordered.

"Just water for me," Asha added before the waiter left.

Some guy came stumbling over. "Damn Dax, you keeping this choice piece of woman to yourself?"

Asha recognized him immediately from the team. Jethro Perkins. Defensive Lineman.

Dax rolled his eyes. "We're working Perkins."

"I'll bet you are. When you're done, send her over my way. You know I love a little spicy Latina."

"Perkins, you're an asshole. This is Asha Wix. She works for the team."

Perkins frowned. "Wix isn't a Latin name?"

Asha spoke through clenched teeth. She was not in the mood to play the game of 'what are you?' right now. "Perkins, if you don't mind, I'd love to finish my meeting with Dax. And no, I'm not Latin. I'm Persian."

Perkins eyes went wide. "Oh snap. Princess Jasmine. I get it. You got the whole outfit and everything at home? Or is that part of your act?"

Asha wasn't a violent person, but her hand twitched with the urge to smack him. First, did he really have no idea how ignorant he sounded? Second, the way he was talking, it sounded like he thought she was a —she whipped her attention toward Dax. "Does he think I'm a hooker?"

Perkin's dark blond brows lifted. "You mean you're not a hooker?"

Dax stood. "Okay, we're done here. First you owe Asha an apology for being an asshole."

"Fuck, man. I didn't mean anything by it. How was I supposed to know she wasn't a pro? Half the girls in the VIP room are. Or at least strippers."

Dax gripped Perkins' shoulder tightly, and the other man winced. "Just say the words, 'I'm sorry I was a dickhead. I'm going to my own table now.'"

Perkins muttered the words before slinking off. Asha blinked up at Dax. "You didn't need to do that. I can handle myself. I did grow up with Damon as a brother."

"I know." His voice was back to level. "But he was all kinds of out of line." Dax watched her closely. She knew he'd taken in her full appearance at the door, but now he studied her face intently.

She cleared her throat. "So, I thought we could start with discussing your current image," Asha said, diving right in.

He sat back, lounging in his chair. "Okay. What about it?"

"How exactly would *you* describe it?" She leaned forward, propping her head into her palm. Dax's gaze flickered down toward her chest, then back to her face quickly.

"Does it matter what I think?" he evaded deftly.

Uh-uh, you don't get to hide from me. "It matters to me. I want to know how much thought you've put into how you present yourself to people, and *why* you choose to give people this particular impression."

His brows furrowed deeper. "Aren't you supposed to just tell me what to do?" He shifted in his seat, his gaze flickering uncomfortably around the room.

Asha reached across the table, selected an olive from the tiny bowl, and popped it into her mouth. After chewing thoughtfully for a moment, she said, "I can *try* telling you what to do, I'm bossy by nature. But I was watching your practice today, and I've seen footage from practices with Coach Moore. I know that *telling* you what to do and you actually doing it are worlds apart." She shrugged. "So I figured I'd ask if you like your current image, or if you want to change it."

Dax laughed, some of the tension leaving his shoulders. "Okay. What's my current image? I guess... Legacy kid. Runs in the family... lazy, playboy, partier. I like to have a good time, which I can do because I'm a Coulter. Football's in my blood. I *sometimes* live up to the hype, but most of the time...I'm a disappointment. But, hey, I've gotta be something, right? And my sibs, Bryce and Echo, already have their little niches so, why not make screwup mine?" He shrugged, averting his gaze as he spoke. But he didn't look away fast enough.

She could see a familiar flash of pain in his eyes, along with a desire to keep it private. Swallowing uncomfortably, Asha sidestepped. They'd have plenty of time for the dark and uglies. "So, what would you like for your image to be?"

Dax rolled his eyes, but was saved from having to answer by the appearance of the waiter with their drinks and Dax's order of stuffed mushroom caps.

Popping one in his mouth and signaling for Asha to help herself, he spoke around the food. "I want my image to be whatever the organization wants it to be. I'm a team player. Or at least I will be, once you beat me into submission. Tell me what to do, and I'll do my best."

"Yeah, that doesn't really seem to jive with what I've seen," she laughed wryly.

"Well then, I suppose it's your job to figure out a way to motivate me to change." His tone was half question, half challenge. "Unless, of course, the guys upstairs decide I'm more marketable in my current state. Everyone loves watching a train wreck." The grin he gave her was salacious, but there was something behind his eyes. As if he were reading from the pre-approved bad-boy script.

"I suppose I have my work cut out for me, then." Asha took a long sip from her water.

Suddenly, someone banged on the Plexiglas wall to her left and she jumped, splashing her water all down her front. *Shit.* Dax turned to acknowledge the fans that had found him, giving a little wave and thumbs up as they pulled out their phones to snap a few pictures.

There were some muffled shouts, a lewd offer from a blond girl with a laughing group of friends, and some shouted questions about just what he and Asha were planning on doing to each other that night.

Asha flushed. Dax just shook his head, as if he was used to all this. It didn't even faze him. She patted her dress with a handful of napkins. After a moment, Dax met her gaze and did an excellent job of keeping his eyes on her face.

"This, right here, would be a good place to start thinking about doing things differently," she said.

Clearing his throat, he looked away again, and shifted in his seat. "You don't have to worry about them taking pictures," he told her, offering her his own napkin. "The windows here are notoriously bad for using a flash. Anything they get will be blurry as hell. Just enough to use to tell a story at a party, but nothing they could turn around and sell, or anything."

Asha stopped wiping her dress when the group moved back out to the dance floor, and Dax's attention had turned back to her.

"That wasn't what I meant," she explained. "If you're going to come out to a place like this and be seen, that's fine, but you want to control the *way* that you're seen."

"I can't control where and when people take pictures of me

if I'm in public. And I can't be bothered with policing things when someone gets a shot I don't like."

"You can't control others but you *can* control yourself," Asha pointed out. "You can control what you do. For example, the topless dancer in Miami, the naked photo shoot with the model, the drunken antics."

He rolled his eyes. "In other words, don't do anything stupid, don't have fun," he muttered. "Here's the part that you don't understand. All I'm doing is just sitting here with a beautiful woman, but everyone has already made a million assumptions."

She ignored the fluttering in her belly. *Stupid butterflies*. So what if he thought she was beautiful? Getting through to him was going to be harder than she thought. "I would suggest you exercise discretion based on the nature of the environment you put yourself in," Asha continued, trying for politeness. "If you're in a public setting that's as crowded as you say this place gets on the weekend, maybe don't get so wasted you can't remember your own name. Or try not to shout lewd things to security and almost start a riot."

"Oh, I never forget my name, sweetheart. The girl I'm with, sure. But I have Coulter practically tattooed on my soul," Dax muttered darkly. "It's my ticket to everything."

Asha had to close her eyes to keep from laughing. "I think you know what I mean."

He nodded. "I'll keep it in mind."

Maybe a different tactic. They had to get on the same page. Both of their careers depended on it. "How are you liking your new coaches?"

"Oh, no." He shook his head. "It's my turn for questions," he countered and started rapidly firing them off. "Why Jacksonville? Are you liking the job so far? And are there any guys on the team who need a talking-to about how they're treating you?" He frowned when he asked that last question.

"Okay, that's way more than I asked you, and mine were for work," she argued, reaching for her empty glass of water and frowning. Dax pushed his water glass over for her to take and went back to drinking his beer.

"I promised Damon I'd check on you," he reminded her.

"And my brother isn't in charge of me. If he has questions, he can ask me himself," she snapped.

"Oh," Dax chuckled as he sat forward. "Now *that's* a feeling I recognize. Don't care much for family oversight? Well, welcome to my world."

She wasn't talking about her family. Not with him. "Tell Damon that I'm not discussing my personal life or anything like that, just so you can turn around and tattle on me to him. And I can handle your teammates and whatever comments they might have without you interfering," she lectured.

He laughed. "I guess you can. That's what HR is for, right?"

She didn't laugh. "I think we've done enough work for tonight. Keep what I said in mind, please. It's not just your neck on the line anymore when it comes to your behavior. And if you don't think more about how you come across to the public for your own sake, I *will* take a more hands-on approach."

His brows drew up. "I like the sound of that," he leaned forward. His voice low, he whispered, "Just how hands-on do you plan on getting, Asha?"

What was supposed to happen was, she'd raise a brow and pour her drink on him. *Something.* Something other than flushing deep and feeling her belly pull with need. *Oh, hell no.*

She stood from the table and grabbed her purse. She needed to do something about this response to him. She'd never considered herself particularly sexual. But around Dax, she was all too aware of...everything. His scent, how he moved, *her* body—and how it acted in response to him.

"Sorry," Dax said, reaching out and grabbing her wrist, loosening his grip when she glared at him. "Sorry. Fuck, I'm sorry. I just... It's sort of automatic. I just turn into an asshole sometimes. I'm *sorry*. But you will let me know if there's anything you need, right? If there's anything you don't want getting back to Damon...I won't say anything. Just... You should have someone you can come to if you need something, and I *did* promise Damon, so...I'm here, or whatever. I know it doesn't seem like it right now, but I promise you can count on me."

Her breath caught in her chest. He was being sincere. She could tell by the slight flush on his skin. And his eyes. The startling clarity of those cerulean irises. The words were clearly difficult for him to say, but he did mean them.

She licked her lips, trying not to focus on the way his thumb stroked her wrist. Or, the way her pulse jumped under his touch. "Thank you." She licked her lips again. "And, uh... If *you* need anything, a ride or...whatever, you can always ask me. I mean...it's my job."

He nodded slowly, but his hand still loosely held hers. Driving her slowly mad. "Will do. Thanks for coming out. I guess you were right. We didn't have to do anything this... flashy."

The awkwardness stretched between them until Asha couldn't stand it anymore.

"Well, goodnight then. I'll see you around at work, I'm sure."

"I'll walk you out and get you a car out the back."

"That's not necessary. I'll be—"

He shook his head, cutting her off. "You were seen with me out front. The paparazzi will be waiting."

"Okay. Well, thank you."

Dax ushered Asha to the back of the bar. As they shuffled through the crowd, the only thing she could feel was the warm press of his hand on her back as he guided her. Currents of electricity spread from that spot on her back to the rest of her body.

Holy hell, this was all kinds of inconvenient. *Inconvenient is an understatement, honey.* Her body was responding to him in a way that she'd never felt before, and it was more than inconvenient. More like a disaster. She'd felt the pull of attraction earlier today, and naïvely, she thought she'd be able to ignore it. Shove it under the rug. No such luck.

Dax was a professional athlete. That meant he went through women like Kleenex. And an uptight virgin was not going to get his attention for very long. Not like she'd intended to still be a virgin at twenty.

Okay, so maybe she hadn't really done anything about that fact, either. She figured it would happen someday. But someday got replaced with studying, and doing everything in her power to gain her father's love. She hadn't really had time for boys.

Oh, and her brother was Damon Wix, so most guys avoided her, for fear he'd annihilate them.

At the back door, Dax spoke to one of the security guards, who then nodded and went outside.

"They'll get you a cab, and let you know when it's here."

She blinked up at him and cleared her throat. "Thank you. You didn't have to do the knight-in-shining-armor thing, but it's appreciated."

"Well, you were my dat—uh, meeting, person, thing, so... uh..." He sighed. "You came with me, so I'm making sure you get home safe. Look at me being the good guy."

And just as soon as the sincerity was there, it was quickly driven out. Not to worry; now that she knew it was there, lurking under the surface, she knew she could get it back.

Luckily, the hallway wasn't as crowded as the VIP area or the main club, but a mix of busboys, security, and wait staff ran back and forth at a quick clip. One of them bumped her, shoving her into Dax's big body. Thanks to his quick reflexes, he steadied her in an instant, only for her to realize that her body was pressed against his like a plaster mold.

Dax stared down at her, his eyes going darker. More focused. His lips parted, and Asha couldn't control the wild swing of her erratic heartbeat. Low in her belly, something hot and slick pulled at her, making her want...things. Things with him. Things she had no business wanting. Her nipples pebbled to hard peaks against his chest, as she fought for breath.

Luckily, she wasn't the only one affected. Even as his pupils dilated, his breath came out in choppy spurts. When he finally spoke, his voice was low, rough. "Asha—" It was part question, part, *I'm going to do very dirty things to you*. Or, maybe that was just in her head.

He leaned his head down, and for a moment, Asha dared to breathe, dared to hope—

"Hey, Coulter, got that cab for you."

In a flash, Dax set her away from him, and Asha's head swam as she tried to focus. He licked his lips and took a very deliberate step back. "Let's get you safely in a cab, yeah?"

Even as he shut the cab door behind her, Asha couldn't help but wonder, what the fuck had just happened?

DAX'S LEGS SHOOK AS HE STUMBLED BACK TO HIS TABLE. *What. The. Fuck?* Whatever the hell that was with Asha, he was pretty sure it wasn't what Damon was looking for. Shit, all she did was breathe on his neck, and he'd gone rigid. Oh, and newsflash, he was still fucking hard. The whisper of his name on her lips... That was like an invitation to dream up all the ways he could make her say it.

He needed to clear his head. Asha Wix was not at all what he'd expected. All prim one moment, walking sex appeal the next. He needed to get laid, and quick. The sooner he forgot her, the better. It had been a hell of a day. Her appearance that morning, and then the new coaches in the afternoon. They were just more disruptive changes to what little routine had already been established in the weeks of training camp, preseason games, and finally, the first two weeks of regular season games.

Asha's about-face though—it could give him a second chance, maybe. It wasn't that he *wanted* to be the fuckup. It was just his role. And, like a moron, he'd slipped into it with her. Had he really hit on Damon's sister? *You. Are. An. Asshole.* Well, someone needed to tell him some shit he didn't already know. It didn't matter that his dick had been as hard as steel since meeting her that morning. He wasn't going there. Besides, he had a feeling she had a type, and football player wasn't it.

Maybe she could do what he couldn't on his own. He wanted the acknowledgment that he was good enough for the endorsements on his own. She could help. But first, he needed to stop being a dick—and a horny dick, at that.

He could still feel the effects of Asha's mesmerizing gaze. The determination and strength in her eyes were disconcerting. She was tough, but also not judgmental like most people. She didn't back down, either. And when her body had been flush against his, her beautiful, dark eyes had shifted from tempered to melted chocolate, warm and inviting. He could fall into those depths... Except, he wouldn't.

Because...Damon's sister. So, there was that. His best friend trusted him. And even Dax wasn't that much of a fuckup.

The blonde from earlier was back in front of him before he could notice her approach and take evasive measures. He didn't want to talk to fans tonight, especially not groupie fans. Besides, she wasn't the woman on his mind.

"My ex was a huge fan of yours," she shouted near his ear.

Dax nodded politely and paid his tab. He wasn't feeling this anymore. He hadn't really wanted to go out in the first place. He'd sort of just wanted the opportunity to make Asha squirm.

"My offer still stands," she continued with a suggestive wink, before moving off toward the side of the dance floor, where the corridor with the bathrooms stood.

He didn't want her. But Asha was in no way available. And he had a hell of a hard-on. Maybe this was what he needed to get her out of his head. The asshole on his shoulder stretched. He switched off his thinking brain and crossed the floor to follow the blonde, glancing over his shoulder to make sure no one was paying attention.

The guilt that surfaced was unfamiliar. He didn't want to go do something stupid after the conversation he and Asha had just had. *But this isn't stupid. You're releasing the tension. It's just a workout.*

Guilt churned in his belly. The blonde turned and nuzzled his neck. His mind offered up an image of Asha doing the same.

It wasn't *really* a betrayal of Damon's trust if all he did was *think* about Asha, right? *Acting* on it *with* Asha, making a move on her, that was where the line was... Or at least, that's what he told himself as he followed the blond woman into the handicapped stall and let her push him up against the wall, the metal handrail catching him at the base of his spine. *This is stupid.* The Dax he could be spoke from somewhere inside. The Dax he was shoved the better version into a darkened closet.

The blonde in front of him had a fiery determination that alcohol had fanned into a full-blown blaze. She knelt and worked to unfasten the buckle of his belt.

"So, you're getting back at your ex," Dax muttered, as he braced his hands on the support bar. The blond stranger had worked his pants and boxers down his thighs far enough to expose his erection. Which oddly, had started to subside. She began to stroke him. But shit, the more she touched him, the worse it got.

"He went and fucked my friend. So I'm going to ruin you for him," she said. Dax squeezed his eyes shut and tried to concentrate. He wasn't getting harder. *Shit.* Why was this happening?

"Easy there," he grunted. "Just...give me a sec."

Oh, God. He couldn't get it up? *Him?*

The blonde, with her tits pushed up to her chin and her skirt so tight he could tell the pattern of her underwear, was having the exact opposite effect he wanted. He'd always gone for the easy lay. The easy way out. Now what? He wanted prim and proper? Though, Asha'd hardly been that tonight. *Fuck.* He leaned his head back against the cool tile of the bathroom wall, and tried not to notice when his hair caught on something sticky.

He tried to focus on anything but the blonde. Jen. Jen was safe, but his brain wouldn't conjure her image.

A sudden, frustrated squeeze from the blonde startled him back to the image of Asha as she walked away in that fitted fuchsia dress.

And what do you know? That did the trick. His cock stirred back to life, and the blonde made some small noise to celebrate her victory before she took a solid hold of him and bent her head to take him into her mouth.

Dax poured all his focus on the sensations triggered by her tongue, her teeth, the warm slide of her mouth. And then he tripped over the no-go line. Picturing Asha's dark locks over her shoulder as she licked the length of him. Gently teasing the head of his dick. The thoughts of her full lips moving over his stiff length. Her wrist had been so soft. Was she that soft everywhere? Her neck, her belly, her inner thighs? The longing to touch her, to know what the pressure of her hand in his felt like, to brush a hand across the soft waves of her dark hair.

Suddenly, the blonde changed her technique.

"Easy, easy," he grunted, taking a firmer hold of her sticky, hairsprayed locks to slow her down. "Take your time. No rush."

She slowed, and he loosened his grip on her head to take hold of the railing again. Her hair either had too much product in it, or it had been dyed too many times. It was brittle to the touch.

He wanted soft strands, and went back to imagining the texture of Asha's hair, thick and loose around her shoulders, the way she brushed it out of her face so she could keep him fixed in her sights.

Picturing her hair brushing his thighs as she sucked him was enough to take him over the edge.

Locked in the fantasy of Asha, her silken hair and her hot mouth, tingling started in the base of his spine. He imagined Asha smiling playfully at him, as he slid a hand up her silky thigh, pushing the fabric of that fuchsia dress up along with it.

The smile she gave him sent him into free-fall. As waves of pleasure washed over him, he knew two things were certain. First, he was an asshole. Second, Asha Wix was going to be a problem for him. Dax rested his head against the wall, his eyes focused on the ceiling instead of anywhere near the blonde kneeling in front of him. He knew, bone-deep, that as much as he might be tempted by Asha Wix—she was off-limits.

EIGHT

Asha fought to focus through Monday morning's staff meeting.

"Considering the changes made to the coaching staff, and the limited time the boys have had to adjust, I think we played pretty damn well. But we still lost," Adams rattled on. "And while it's going to take some time to evaluate the long-term impact of these changes, we need to do everything we can to bring attendance and ticket sales back up. People see a full stadium, and they know it's somewhere they want to be. Folks leaving halfway through the game, they figure why bother shelling out that kind of dough to be disappointed. We're lucky at the moment," he continued, pacing at the front of the group, "because we're heading into a stretch of road games. We won't be back here for close to a month, and that gives us some time to change people's minds. To get them reinvested in our team and our prospects. Even if they lose, we want them to support us, and to *want to* support us, no matter what."

There were nods of agreement around the room, accompanied by looks of hesitant anticipation.

"For this upcoming road trip, you're going to be traveling

with the team." The announcement was met with a number of poorly contained sighs and other sounds of displeasure, but Adams pressed on. "We don't want the connections you're building with the players to fall apart because you're not going to be able to see them regularly over the next four weeks," he explained. "If there are concerns that arise, I want you there to handle them personally. That way if anything happens, we have a better shot at controlling the story."

Adams' gaze lingered on Asha. She knew that Dax was one of the most likely candidates when it came to causing trouble on the road. Of course, she would have the problem child. Mr. Sexy-as-Sin was the reason she hadn't been able to sleep all weekend.

She only had to do a quick search of his college football career online to find photos of him doing keg-stands and other ridiculous antics with some of his teammates. So many photos. Something about being at home appeared to be sacred to him, while traveling seemed to give him the uncontrollable impulse to make his presence felt.

Though it's probably just practicality, she thought as Adams continued with his lecture about expectations for their coming travels. *Can't make a nuisance of yourself at home, or you won't have anywhere left to go.*

While many of her colleagues were disappointed or annoyed by the prospect of traveling for the job, Asha found it exciting. Of course, she didn't have anyone waiting at home while she traipsed off to essentially babysit a grown-ass man.

She dragged her attention back to the meeting. Or tried to. She'd be attached at the hip to Dax for weeks. That meant weeks of him potentially touching her wrist. Who knew the wrist was an erogenous zone? She sure as hell hadn't. She couldn't even put on perfume this morning without thinking of him. Or the pain in his eyes as he apologized. Or worse, the way his arms had snapped around her. The stark hunger on his face. The press and throb of his erection against her belly. Oh, man. She was so totally screwed.

There goes rule number three.

"Anyone late for practice will be benched for the first drive of the game—offense or defense, it doesn't matter," Coach Mills informed the players. His eyes found Dax in the gathered players. Dax barely concealed his smirk; his reputation from his college days wasn't going to be forgotten anytime soon. "I want to know where you all are at all times," Mills continued. "That *doesn't* mean carrying your phone around and making sure it's charged so I can get ahold of you *if* I need to. It means I want you to check in *before* you go anywhere. Don't text or leave a message and hope I get it; if you don't receive confirmation or permission, you stay put. If you can't follow instructions *off* the field, I'm going to assume you can't follow them *on* the field, either. Understood?"

No one was going to enthusiastically cheer for such strict measures, but it appeared Coach Mills took their silence as agreement and continued. "Lastly, the bosses upstairs are really pushing this PR arrangement hard. Your shadows are coming with us. Lucky you. They will be going with you just about everywhere, not only to keep an eye on you, but to also 'get to know you better'. If you want this thing to go away, you have to convince the bosses that it isn't necessary, not go out of your way to screw it up as a way of showing them that it isn't going to work. If you show them you can handle yourselves, that you know how grown men should behave and act accordingly, maybe they'll call off their watchdogs and let us all get back to the business of playing football. How does that sound?"

There was a bit more enthusiasm from the players this time around, and they muttered their agreement to the prospect of getting rid of their PR buddies.

Dax remained silent. It was possible he was the only one who didn't really mind having a shadow. He'd stopped being such an ass once he and Asha'd found some common ground. Or maybe more truthfully, once he started to remember that Damon was his friend and had asked for a favor. Yeah, he couldn't get her out of his head. His shower activities were evidence of that. *But*, she was smart and knew her football. She was also surprisingly funny. Go figure. Once they were able to relax a bit, they actually were able to talk and shit. Just as long as he didn't think about her touching him while he was with her. Then it was more difficult to…just talk.

She was also some kind of sports trivia nut. Her knowledge was incredible and went deeper than just the Coulter family…or even football in general.

He wasn't sure how he felt about having her along for the upcoming road trip, though. He didn't mind, *exactly*. He liked her. The problem was, he just *liked* her a little too much.

Their next game was against San Diego, which meant he'd be playing at home. The calls and voicemails had already started rolling in. *Will you come for dinner while you're here? We need to get together to go over details for the wedding. Gramps has box seats so we'll be at the game.*

Then, the most important thing to consider… Would he have to bring Asha along? He wasn't sure how she'd handle meeting his family. Or having to explain to them the hows and whys of that particular work situation. He could already hear the jokes about him needing a babysitter, and everyone offering her tips on how to get him to do things, or worse, *asking* for tips on how she managed him.

Yeah, Asha and his family, not okay. Besides, he didn't want anyone else around to witness the black sheep slaps. He could do without having an audience there. Except, on the other hand, maybe if she was there, they'd back off. Give him some breathing room. Maybe it wasn't such a bad idea, after all. He just had to keep from touching her. How hard could that be?

IN THE END, IT WAS MUCH EASIER THAN DAX EXPECTED.

"Is Wix joining you?" Coach Mills had asked when Dax approached him at the end of practice with his request.

"I already spoke with her about it," Dax explained.

"Fine. Just be back at your hotel by ten. Practice starts at nine tomorrow morning."

"Yes, sir," Dax nodded before heading to take off his pads and hit the showers.

Inside the locker room, a few of his teammates were grumbling about the curfew and figuring out what to do to fill their free time. They still had another day of practice before the game, and some had been looking to spend the *night* out on the town, not the *afternoon*. Most of them were running into resistance from their PR shadows. Granted, this was San Diego, and bikini-clad women were everywhere. So there were plenty of opportunities to get into trouble.

"My guy is paired up with three of us," Thomlinson was whispering to Samuels. "He can't be in three places at once. What're we supposed to do with that?"

Mitchell elbowed Dax. "What about you? You taking your PR chick out? Or d'you think having her around'll scare off the others? I've never met someone so uptight." He laughed, and a few of the guys who overheard laughed and chuckled, too.

"Oh, I don't get to have fun." Dax clutched a hand to his chest in mock horror. "I've gotta head out to my parents' place for a family thing. And yes, she has to come with me." He didn't like the way they talked about her. *Shut it. That was you a week ago.*

"Introducing her to the folks, huh?" Thomlinson chuckled. "Sounds pretty serious to me."

The last place he'd take anyone he wanted to keep would be to that firing squad. "Any woman I chose to get serious with, I'd keep as far away from that crew as possible," Dax said with a laugh. "Seriously, though, my brother's getting married in a few weeks, so it'll probably be wedding stuff the whole time. Not fun."

"What about the rest of us?" Samuels asked. "When do *we* get to meet the family?"

"After Sunday's game, probably," he muttered. Despite the fact that all of them were actually playing football professionally, they were still awed by his family. Normally they treated him like any other player, but it was moments like this. Times when he saw the eagerness behind the joking, that reminded Dax that when it came to his pedigree, they all looked at him differently. "Heading out. Gotta find my shadow before we can leave for the 'burbs." He moved quickly out of the group and headed for the door.

Asha was waiting outside his hotel room, ready to go, when he arrived to drop off his bag and change.

"You're wearing that?" he couldn't help asking, leaving the door open for her to follow him in so she didn't have to stand in the hallway while he finished getting ready.

She frowned and looked down at her grey pencil skirt and royal-blue satin blouse.

"You look like you're interviewing for a job," he said as he pulled things out of the suitcase he'd packed.

"Well...I wasn't sure how formal this dinner thing would be, and I didn't want to be *under*dressed," Asha stammered as she smoothed the fabric of her skirt. "Besides, I technically *am* working."

What he didn't say, was that the prim getup gave him naughty-teacher fantasies. *Not. Helpful.*

Dax took a pair of khakis and a loose button-up shirt to the bathroom to change, calling over his shoulder to Asha. "Yeah, I'm not going to be telling them that part of it."

Asha was waiting for him with a furrowed brow, her arms crossed over her more than ample chest when he emerged again. "Please tell me you weren't going to tell them we're dating or anything."

He laughed, even as something burned in his gut. "No, though it might be worth it to see the looks on some of their faces," he said, laughing again. "They'd never believe it."

"So then, what *are* you going to tell them?"

"The truth, insomuch as it applies. You're Damon's little sister." As he bent over at the edge of the bed to put on his shoes, he just barely caught the way her jaw clenched and eyes rolled when he said that. "You're working with the team now and got sent along on this road trip. That I thought you might like getting away from it for a while, and didn't want to be on your own. Something along those lines."

Asha's brows rose. "I think I might be rubbing off on you," she mused. "You've at least picked up a bit about how to frame a situation for your audience."

He laughed. "You didn't teach me that," he told her. "Years of living with my family taught me that."

"So we'll see how much of it is my doing when it comes to your handling of the public, then." Asha shrugged as she reached into her purse for the keys to her rental car.

"Mind if I drive?" Dax offered, holding his hand out to take the keys. "I do know where I'm going better than you do."

"You drive out, I'll drive back," she insisted. "From how you talk about your family, I'm guessing you'll be drinking while you're there."

"Aw, you're getting to know me deep down," he said with a sarcastic grin, and was rewarded with her smile. For several frozen beats he simply stared. What the hell was this girl doing to him?

NINE

"And how is your brother liking New England?" Brent Coulter asked, as he ushered Dax and Asha into the sitting room, where his wife offered them drinks.

"He seems to like it. Damon has never been one for the cold. He's like my mom. We grew up in Hawaii. So we'll see how he does," Asha told him as she accepted a glass of iced tea from Julia. "It's a bit intense and there's a lot of pressure, but he responds well to that. I know he misses blocking for Dax," she said, turning to him and trying to pass the conversation onto him.

"I think I met your brother once or twice. Obviously, I'm familiar with your father and his work with the league." Rory Coulter jumped in, from his spot on an overstuffed loveseat. His wife sat beside him, sipping a cocktail. "Not the least bit surprised when New England snapped him up. Wish the Steelers had had the sense to do it first," he laughed.

Next to her, Dax stiffened, but he kept his mouth shut.

"What exactly is it you do with the Thrashers then, Ashley?" Julia asked, as she brought a beer to Dax.

"It's Asha," she corrected.

"I'm so sorry about that, dear. Ethnic names aren't my specialty. It's a beautiful name."

Dax exhaled slowly.

Asha knew this wasn't a fight worth picking. "Don't worry," she reassured the older woman. "You're not the first to call me that, and you won't be the last." *Unfortunately.* Hell, she looked straight-up Persian. No one would ever guess her father was white. *Breathe deep. It's only for a couple of hours.*

"Won't be the last what?" Echo asked as she breezed into the room, stopping at her father's chair to give him a quick half hug then pouncing on her mother with a peck on the cheek. She ended up at the bar in the corner, where she started fixing her own rum and cola.

"Asha, this is my twin sister, Echo," Dax said.

"Oh, so *this* is Asha," Echo said with a teasing glance to Dax, who rolled his eyes. "It's very nice to finally meet you. Dax has not been forthcoming with any details about you."

"Uh, nice to meet you, too." This was Dax's twin? They looked nothing alike.

"Yes, *this* is Asha. Damon's sister." His tone was mocking to match Echo's. Then he quickly changed the subject. "Where're Bryce and Tami?"

"They should be here soon, but they'll probably have to cut out as soon as dinner's over. They have to go meet with the manager at the country club to iron out some of the arrangements," Echo said, clapping gleefully. "Only six weeks to go."

"Our oldest son and his fiancée are getting married in November," Julia said for Asha's benefit. "They just won their first US Open title for mixed doubles."

Asha nodded with polite interest, though anyone who paid even the slightest bit of attention to the sports news cycle was well aware of both those facts.

"What about Fox and Gage?" Dax asked.

"Gage is working on his college applications." His father said.

From the little Asha had heard from Dax's parents so far, she knew they were proud of their children's abilities and accomplishments, but there was something special about the tone with which Brent spoke about his youngest son.

"Hasn't he already got a dozen scholarship offers?" Dax scoffed. He turned to Asha to add, "Gage is on the high school basketball team. They've been scouting him since his freshman year."

That's right, Asha thought, as she nodded with understanding. *Brent played basketball, too.*

"He still needs to make his formal applications. And Fox... well, he'll show up as soon as the food's on the table."

There was a commotion from the main hall, and everyone craned their necks to see Bryce and Tami come through the front door into the foyer. Julia greeted them before excusing herself to go let the cook, Fox, and Gage all know they'd be sitting down to eat in a few minutes.

"Sorry we're late," Tami apologized quickly as she and Bryce glanced around the room.

Asha suddenly found herself at the center of attention again, when they both stared curiously at her. "Hi. I'm Damon's little sister," she said, reluctantly falling back on the easiest explanation.

"Damon?" Tami looked to Bryce.

"My best friend from college," Dax piped up, rising from his seat and holding a hand out to help Asha up as well. "We were on the same team, and now *Asha* and *I* are on the same team."

"I'm in the public relations and marketing department for the Thrashers," she said, shaking Tami's hand while the two oldest Coulter brothers engaged in that weird shoulder clap all the Coulter men seemed fond of using to greet one another. "I'm traveling with the team this road trip, and Dax thought it would be nice to give me the chance to escape my colleagues for a while."

Tami studied her closely. "That was...*nice* of Dax to bring you along."

Asha swallowed hard. "Yeah. That Dax. Forever nice."

Tami looked back and forth between them, and Asha flushed. She might have fooled the rest of the family, but Tami knew. Fantastic. Bryce handed his brother a drink, and Dax threw it back like a thirsty man.

Asha sighed. She certainly had her work cut out for her tonight.

TEN

Shoot him now. Dax was already one Scotch in, thanks to his brother. And thanks to his grandparents, he was working his way through the second. So far, he'd counted almost five off-color or racially insensitive remarks. Which, knowing his grandfather, was actually pretty good. The one he'd been surprised by was from his grandmother.

Everyone was incredibly polite during dinner, but he couldn't help but stiffen whenever someone directed a question toward him. He was good at game talk, though. *Never reveal anything. Keep it surface.* Thankfully, most of the discussion centered on Bryce and Tami's wedding preparations.

Asha handled it with grace. And a few times, she'd taken his hand under the table and given him a gentle squeeze to keep him from saying anything. More than once, he willed her to hold on just a little longer.

"So, why do you need to go in person to the country club tonight?" Echo asked.

"We can't decide how we want the tables arranged," Bryce said. "We need to see the space we're working with in person. It's like... working with building blocks."

"More like dominoes," Tami added. "We can't really settle on the seating arrangements until we know how the tables are going to be laid out, which, according to the wedding planner, also affects the flower arrangements somehow—"

"And the photographer and videographer will have to work around them, as well." Bryce picked up Tami's thread of the conversation.

"I don't understand all this fuss about a wedding," Fox muttered between mouthfuls.

They all just ignored Fox as Bryce continued. "It'll all be easier to figure out if we have some help. Like family help, I mean."

"Not Gage," Brent overruled before his youngest son could speak for himself either way. "You need to finish those applications. The deadlines are coming up soon, and you know they coincide with tryouts and your team's first practices."

There was a flash of irritation in Gage's expression, but as usual, his baby brother said nothing. Poor kid probably had other plans and zero interest in spending his Friday night getting caught up in wedding planning. But the fact he was now forbidden from going immediately made the idea appealing.

"I'm game," Echo volunteered quickly. "I'll give Jen a call, too. She was talking about looking for something to do tonight."

Fuck. Jen? With Asha right here? Together? His skin prickled with heat. Which was ridiculous, because there was nothing going on with Asha. Except for the masturbation habit he'd developed.

"I doubt this is what she had in mind," Dax quipped weakly.

"Do you *not* want me to invite her?" Echo met his gaze, her eyes full of challenge. She was fucking with him.

"Of course you can invite her," he said carefully. "I just don't think you should be surprised if she says no." Yeah, he was fooling nobody. Fuck, he was so screwed. *Shit.* Why was it so damn hot in here?

"How 'bout you, Fox?" Bryce prodded. "It'll be fun."

"The bunch of us in an empty room standing in for tables and guests while you and Tami use us like puppets?" Fox lips twisted into a sardonic smile. "Why does that not sound like fun?"

"Oh, the room won't be empty. There's some sort of reunion going on tonight. We'll kind of be crashing their party, but the manager said it shouldn't be a problem, so long as we don't make a nuisance of ourselves." Bryce grinned as Fox sat up with a smile. "What kind of reunion?"

As it turned out, it was a local high school's tenth reunion, and there turned out to be more than a few no-shows. Fox was in heaven with all the available older women in the building.

Dax couldn't help but keep an eye on Asha. She'd handled the relative formality of his family just fine, but in the new social situation, she was stiffer...more awkward. She kept looking over her shoulder, as though someone was going to come up behind them at any moment to physically remove them from the premises.

As they waited in the foyer of the club for both Jen and the manager to meet them, Dax nudged Asha and nodded his head in the direction of the name tag table. "We could always do this undercover," he joked.

Asha giggled and smacked his arm. "I doubt it would help the situation if someone spotted the lot of you."

"You're here, too," he pointed out. "Whatever happens to us, happens to you. *Our* fates are forever intertwined."

"I'm not a Coulter. *Nobody* wants pictures of me."

His gaze swept over her. Even in the prim skirt and blouse, with those heels, she looked amazing. Classy. He wanted to make her...*less classy*. "I doubt that."

She ignored him. "And if that does happen, and a story about you crashing a high school reunion goes viral, it'll be *my* ass on the line at work," Asha emphasized.

"Oh, Coach Mills would be sure to punish me in practice, rest assured," Dax promised. "And, if anything, it would give you the perfect means for demonstrating your skills. Say it goes viral. First of all, I'm not the only Coulter here. And with Bryce *and* Tami here, they'd be the real story. Second, the club here would put out a statement that I'm sure you would help them write. Explaining how we aren't, in fact, *crashing* the event, but are here in regards to my brother's approaching wedding."

"The press does love a good love story," Asha agreed.

"And in that case, I'm here not as a troublemaker but as my brother's best man. My opinions on these matters are vital to the success of this wedding."

They both laughed at that. God, she was pretty when she smiled. "Hey, so I was think—" But he didn't finish the thought. Out of the corner of his eye, he spotted Jen. He immediately put distance between him and Asha, stepping forward to give Jen a quick hug. Was it weird he didn't get that same spark of insta-lust when he touched Jen? Whatever. Asha was clouding his brain.

"Jen, this is Asha Wix. She does PR for the team and I played with her brother in college. Asha, this is Jen Atwood. She's a longtime family friend." The hairs on the back of his neck stood at attention, and he could practically *feel* Echo watching him. More than once, when he showed interested in someone new, she'd call asking him all about his flavor of the week. It was disconcerting how she could sense it.

"It's a pleasure to meet you," Asha said with a sunny smile. Great. Of course Asha was being nice to her. The woman he was currently obsessed with—who he shouldn't be obsessed with, and who he couldn't have—making nice with the woman who was supposed to be his future...someday. Maybe. One day. Totally normal. Not stress-inducing at all.

As the manager let them in, Jen turned to Echo and started chatting.

Bryce and Tami followed the manager for a few minutes. Echo started angling herself and Jen toward him and Asha, and he knew an ambush was imminent. As the three women spoke, he tried to take part in the conversation, but he was too aware of Asha. The way she moved, the way she angled her head. More than once, Jen or Echo asked him a question, and he was busy staring at Asha.

Jen, dipshit. Jen is the prize.

"It was good of you to agree to help with this," he said quietly, while Echo and Fox were busy playing twenty questions with Asha.

"I didn't have anything better to do on a Friday night," Jen shrugged. "What does that say about me, huh?"

"Still, this'll be fun. Now that you're here." Lame. Why did he sound so lame?

Jen came close to snorting with laughter. "Please, please stop, Dax," she begged. "It's a joke that's gone on way too long. *You*, pretending to hit on *me*."

He frowned. *What?* Pretending? He had game. So much game. "What if I'm not joking?"

Her brows shot up. "Not joking?"

He rolled his eyes. "Okay, what if I want to *stop* joking?"

She crossed her arms. "Can I ask you a question?"

"Sure."

"Do you even *like* me?"

Huh? "Of course, I like you."

"No, I mean in a meaningful way. Are you even attracted to me?"

He flushed. What was she asking? "Of course. You know you're beautiful."

"Yes, Dax, I'm pretty. But do you actually *feel* anything for me? Or do you just think it would be a great idea to date me? I'm safe. In with the fam."

"I—" He frowned slightly.

"Because since I've been here, you can't seem to take your eyes off of Asha. And you have *never* looked at me like that."

This conversation was getting away from him. "She's just a friend. More like my friend's sister."

"You look at her with more heat and interest than you ever have with me. I adore you, but I want to be with someone who *looks* at *me* that way. And not just because I'm a good idea." She patted him on the chest and walked away to join a laughing Asha and Echo.

Dax followed behind, kicking himself for managing to royally screw up that conversation. She didn't know what she was talking about. Except, if he really stopped to think about it, she was right. He thought she was beautiful, but she didn't pull at that part of him. He *loved* women, so of course, he wanted her. But she had a point. She didn't occupy his mind. Didn't keep him up at night. Asha did. And that was just one big problem.

"You okay? You seem tense," Asha asked.

He nodded stiffly. "Fine."

"Well, come on, then." Asha pulled him out toward the edge of the dance floor. "If we're going to crash this party and risk our necks, let's do it right."

His lips twitched. "You like to dance?"

"Don't let my good-girl look fool you. I *love* to dance."

The DJ was only playing songs that came out during the high school years of the reunion attendees. Clusters of people filled the dance floor. Some were moving halfheartedly, still afraid after all those years to look foolish in front of the cool kids, while the majority seemed to be truly enjoying themselves. Asha dragged him to the edge of the dance floor. Someone bumped into her, pushing her into him. Repeating the way they'd been pressed together at the club.

Oh, God. Her soft body pressed deliciously against him. She smelled so good... She stumbled back a step and he held his breath. Her pupils dilated. Shit. Could she feel this too? "Asha—"

The voice of the deejay came over the speakers, cutting him off, looking for the class prom king and queen to share a dance in the center of the floor and the music softened.

Dax held his breath. She felt so damn good in his arms. It seemed like she was holding her breath too, but when she finally exhaled, her body melded to his. For several moments they danced to the music, him more than hyper aware of how close they were. He could kiss her she was so close.

His gaze pinned on her lips, and he wanted to slide his tongue over her bottom lip. But then, she suddenly backed away and cleared her throat.

"We should uh...we should go find the others," Asha suggested, sliding her gaze away from Dax, who still had hold of her hand.

He didn't want to let her go.

"Yeah," Dax agreed, his voice low. He cleared his throat as he stepped back and let go of her hand. "I uh—Echo's over there waving for us. They're probably—"

"We're holding them up," Asha agreed before Dax could finish. "We were supposed to be helping them."

"Right. Let's..." He was in trouble and he needed to find

some way to get her out of his head or he was going to do something really stupid.

"You should be careful with him," Tami said quietly on Asha's right, as Dax went to stand in next to Bryce.

"Oh, don't worry. I've got my eye on him," she answered, without really thinking. "That didn't come out right," she added quickly as Tami laughed beside her. "I just...I mean...Dax didn't want anyone to know this, but... I *had* to come with him tonight. No, literally," she asserted when she saw Tami's good-natured smile shift to confusion. "It's part of my job with the team. We've been paired up with players to help evaluate their behavior and figure out the best ways to manage them. To market them..."

"Ah," Tami blinked. "That must be it, then."

"Must be what?"

"The way he's been reacting to you tonight. He just seems... I'm not the *best* at reading Dax—or any of the Coulters yet, except Bryce, of course—but he seemed to be... Well, I thought he was trying to provoke you, with Jen there—that he was trying to make you jealous," she said.

"Make me jealous," Asha repeated without inflection. That couldn't be right. But maybe that was what she'd felt earlier in the lobby area, while they were waiting for Jen to arrive. She'd been fidgety in a way that was both familiar and foreign—it was similar to the way she felt when an achievement was within reach and she felt threatened.

Perhaps that fidgeting had been more than just worrying about being so close to making it through the night without incident? Maybe it had to do with the warmth that had run through her with Dax's hands on her while they'd been dancing. His strong hands holding her fingers loosely while she twirled, pressed against the small of her back as he reached around to pull her closer to him, the way they rested lightly on her waist... the way those beautiful eyes focused on her like a hawk.

"Guess I was wrong," Tami was saying. "Well—not entirely. He *was* probably trying to provoke you, just not for the reason I thought."

Yes, and why does that bother you so much?

ELEVEN

Right before leaving, Dax pulled Bryce aside.

"You're sure about all this, then?" Dax couldn't help asking Bryce.

"About marrying Tami? Of course I'm sure," Bryce said, laughing. "And it's a little late for you to be having this talk with me, don't you think?"

"No, late would be asking when you're waiting for her at the altar," Dax muttered. "And that's not what I meant. I was talking about me being your best man. Are you sure?"

Bryce's voice softened. "Sorry, Dax—no backing out now."

"At least admit it, all right? Admit that you would have asked Echo first, but Tami called dibs on her."

His brother shook his head. "No. You want to know why I asked you?"

"Yeah."

"Because you were the first person to notice. To care enough to give me the heads-up about the family when Tami and I started. And you're my brother. I love you and shit." He paused, raising an eyebrow at Dax and grinning. "You're not gonna make me hug you now, are you?"

Dax couldn't believe it. Bryce actually *wanted* him as best man? Was it possible he'd looked at their relationship the wrong way all these years?

"Okay. I'll call you about the bachelor party. I need to get out of here."

Bryce nodded. "You okay? You seem off."

"Yeah, I'm fine. Later." All he had to do now was survive the tension in the car with Asha for the next hour.

Asha drove as far over the speed limit as she was comfortable, heading back to the W Hotel downtown. His parents' house was on Rancho Santa Fe, so nearly an hour out of the city. Luckily, it was late enough in the evening for most of the traffic to have cleared, so they made good time.

Aside from a few obligatory comments about how good dinner had been, and that the country club seemed like it would be a wonderful venue for Bryce and Tami's wedding, they rode in silence. But she could practically feel him thinking next to her.

Tami's words of caution haunted Asha. *Be careful with him.* Which way had she meant that? Be careful with him, as in don't hurt *him*? Or be careful *he* didn't hurt *her*?

She shook her head to clear it. It didn't matter how Tami had meant it. To even think about Dax that way was not okay. He wasn't spending time with her because he wanted to. Even if it *was* a possibility. No. No more venturing down fantasy alley, imagining Dax could possibly want her. No more focusing on the way he watched her like a hawk with its prey. And definitely no thinking about what his voice, smile, or laugh could do to her body. She didn't have much experience with guys. Hell, any, really. Dax Coulter was not one to cut her baby teeth on.

Known player, check.

Too good looking for his own good, check.

Football player that could ruin her career, check.

The only man to really make her want to break every single rule she had, check.

She was screwed.

She had a job to do. And the more time they spent together, the closer they got. She was already starting to recognize the way his eyes dimmed when he was confronted with that older version of himself. Or the way his smile in the candid photos of him partying always seemed...artificial. Pasted on, because smiling was simply what you did when someone pointed a camera your way. Truth be told, there were moments of pleasure or enjoyment for him, but mostly what she saw was exhaustion. Someone who had given up trying because he was too used to having people look through him.

She hadn't missed the underlying tension with his family. His parents were okay. A little on the snobbish side, but okay. But Rory, though. *Wow.* What a pompous piece of work. He was so full of bluster, he couldn't see that his grandson idolized him. She couldn't blame Dax for not wanting to go home alone.

When she glanced over at him, watching the world pass by the passenger window, she thought he looked...well, not as lonely as he had a few other times when she'd caught glimpses of him through the night. But relaxed, as if the trial was over.

He caught her watching him in the reflection on the glass and a hint of a smile stretched across his lips. She flushed and turned her attention back to the road.

She needed to reevaluate her tactics with him. There was pain there, and an unspoken pressure. From his family. From himself. He would crack if she didn't help him.

The thought of that happening to him cut her deep. And it was all too close to home.

It was her job to prevent that, and she would do it. So maybe Tami had been right, after all. Maybe she did need to be careful with him.

And she knew the first place to start was going to be with an email she'd received before they'd left the country club...

Dax walked Asha through the doors into the hotel lobby, with only about five minutes to spare. One of Coach Mills' assistants was waiting with a clipboard to cross off the names of the players as they filtered in from their abbreviated evenings.

A number of the players were grumbling among themselves as they headed for the elevators, and there were several who decided they would head to their rooms to change before heading back down to the exercise room or the pool, both of which were open until eleven-thirty.

Dax shrugged off invitations to join them. "Dinner with my family was more than enough to wear me out for the night," he said. "I'll be stewing tonight and working things out on the rest of you in practice."

They laughed as they got off on the players' floor to head to their rooms. Dax hesitated long enough for the doors to close. What was he doing? *You're being a gentleman.* Yeah, right. He just didn't want to leave her side yet.

She didn't say a word as she stepped off the elevator and led the way to her room. They paused in the doorway for a moment before she spoke quietly. "Want a drink?"

"You haven't already demolished your minibar?" he asked with a wry laugh. Fuck yes, he wanted to go in. Hell no, he didn't want a drink.

"Underage, remember? I, uh, have some ideas for you... Marketing-wise," she rushed to add.

The prick of disappointment stung. But of course, she didn't mean she had *those* kinds of ideas for him. That was a pipe dream. Nevertheless, hanging with her was still a better option than sitting alone in his room. He was more apt to get into his head when he saw his family. And that whole thing with Bryce still clanged around in his brain.

"So, that's your family," Asha said as she crossed to the mini-fridge, slipping off her heels as she walked, and retrieved a can of cola and two plastic cups from the tray on top of the dresser. "What's your poison? Rum? Whiskey?"

"Rum," he answered, looking around for a place to sit before opting for the edge of the bed. There was a single chair wedged into the corner by a small table, but that somehow felt too far away.

"One Cuba Libre coming right up."

She grabbed the little bottle and poured it into his cup before adding soda to both cups.

"Yeah, that's my family. Impressed?"

Asha shrugged. "I thought your grandfather would be bigger and your dad would be taller."

Dax chuckled. "That's what you noticed first? I suppose I should be grateful. I remember how big they seemed when I was little. Then I had a growth spurt when I was fourteen and...then not so much."

She handed him the plastic cup with his drink and sat next to him.

"I can see how it must have been hard growing up Coulter."

He took a large gulp of his drink, buying time to get his rising erection under control. *Easy boy. Just a drink and we're out. No one is touching her tonight.* "Most people think I lucked out."

"With that level of scrutiny? I don't envy you on that front. Your dad seems real understanding, though," she added, lightening her tone. "And your mom."

"They were tough, but fair." He felt like he was just feeding her lines from a script, and he hated himself for it. He forced himself to add more. "Even with all my shit, I know they love me."

"I get the tough part, though I'm not always convinced my parents were entirely fair. Especially Dad," Asha said quietly.

His head snapped up. He hadn't expected her to share anything about herself, and it caught him off guard. "It was just you and Damon, right?"

"Yep," Asha confirmed. "The great Damon Wix and the spare."

"I doubt it's like that."

She sighed. "I shouldn't have said that." There was a pause. "Did you play anything else before deciding on football?" she asked, changing the subject. "Did you ever consider something *other* than being an athlete? Or was that frowned upon by your family?"

"You know...I don't think it ever occurred to me to do anything other than football," he admitted. "When I was little, I used to ask Gramps if I could see his Super Bowl ring. It was so big I could fit it over two fingers. I wanted to be just like him, and I always had fun playing football. It was something I could do that Echo wasn't allowed."

"For twins you guys don't seem a lot alike. She looks more like Bryce."

"She's always been closer to him, too. But I dunno, we have this vibe. She's my sister and I love her, but being twins... We were always paired up for things, in the family and out. We were in the same class at school, got invited to the same birthday parties and playdates... I couldn't escape her. And she was always applauded for being so well-behaved, so smart, so thoughtful. I mean she deserved it, don't get me wrong. But Bryce was the same way and I was just...me," he muttered. It was the only way to get attention. He was vaguely aware he was oversharing and that he actually didn't mind. But it was nothing he hadn't told to Damon in college after a bit too much to drink.

"Well, it's no picnic being on the other end. Everyone just takes you for granted. And with my dad, all he cared about was football. Not the fact that I'd skipped three grades, or won a science medal, or things like that. Somehow, no matter what, I still didn't live up to expectations."

"Ever?" He asked, surprised as she kept talking.

"Get an A on one assignment, and if you get a B on the next one, they wonder what happened, what's wrong, why didn't you do as good this time as last time?" she spoke quickly. "So you keep pushing yourself, harder and harder, just to keep from disappointing them, to make them proud."

"I can't even imagine."

"Supposedly I was '*gifted*,'" she explained with mock reverence. "I did well in school at the lower levels, and the teachers wondered if I was being challenged enough. My parents chose to let me advance two grades. I didn't get to see my friends as much—at least, the few who would still talk to me after that. And when it came to my new classmates... I was the youngest, and they already had their little cliques."

"Why didn't you tell your parents you didn't want to?"

Asha gave him a look that made him bite back laughter. "If you had wanted to stop playing football so you could study to be a dentist, how do you think your parents would have taken it?"

The impulse to laugh vanished. "I think they'd have thought it a sound investment, given how many times they had to take Fox in because he'd knocked teeth out during a game," he tried to joke. "But my grandfather..."

"He'd have been disappointed," Asha offered, the stiff confidence of her challenging question replaced by soft uncertainty.

Dax shook his head. "I think he'd have been pleased. Maybe even actually relieved. Me *continuing* in football has been the disappointment. I know I'll never be as good as he was. I mean, look at all he was able to do in his career and *when* he was doing it. He'll always be one of the pillars of the sport. There's no way to compete with that."

"And that's what you've been forced to do, isn't it?" Asha asked. "Compete with your grandfather's legacy."

"That's what it feels like most of the time," he confessed. "Not on the field as much. Sometimes I can stop thinking about what he would do, or how making a certain catch will bring my stats up. When I can get out of my head, it's still fun."

Asha scooted a little closer to him on the bed.

Shit. Shit. Shit. He swallowed hard as danger flags flew upward.

"Then that's what we'll do."

"What is?" He could smell the sweet soda on her breath—or maybe it was from his own breath, mixing with her perfume. He couldn't think. It was like someone had thrown a blanket of fog over him. He leaned in a little closer, swallowing hard and almost forgetting to listen for her answer. If she just turned her head up a bit, or leaned forward, they'd be kissing.

"We stop marketing you based on your name," she answered quietly. "We make an effort to differentiate you from your grandfather. Let you stand out on your own. They've been expecting and encouraging me to get on board with pushing the Coulter brand on the fans...but I'll tell them no. I'll tell them it would be better, for you and for the team, to put some distance from the name. Smack down the comparisons and tell everyone you won't stand for it. Make it about Dax, not Dax *Coulter*." She paused. "Oh, and I have a surprise for you."

"What's that?"

"Come here." She stood and pulled him to the table.

He focused on her delicate feet as she padded across the carpet. Damn, he even thought her feet were hot. He needed help. *Serious* help.

"What's this all about?"

Asha rolled her eyes. "I swear. You must ruin presents all the time." She scrolled to her email and then handed over her iPad.

Dax frowned as he looked at the email. "I don't get it. What am I looking at?"

"I swear." She shook her head and pointed to the lines that mattered, and he scanned them again.

"'Thanks so much for bringing Dax Coulter to our attention,'" he said, reading the email message aloud. "'I spoke to my team, and they'd absolutely love to talk to him regarding an endorsement. He's an amazing athlete, and in line with the Powerfuture brand. Just put us in contact with his agent.'"

He stared for several minutes, unable to process the information. An endorsement? He'd heard of Powerfuture. They did some cool robotics projects. They'd even had a huge Kickstarter campaign for a personal robot. "I don't understand; they want to do a deal with me? They want me to endorse their products? But I'm not technical."

She shook her head. "Doesn't matter. You're edgy, but intelligent. Like them." She shrugged. "I know what happened to the last endorsement. The day I met you, I got to work right away, calling all my contacts to see if anyone had anything that would be mutually beneficial to the both of us. A friend of mine from college came through. She's the director of technology there."

That burning in his chest that had been dogging him for weeks flared sharply. But now, it was accompanied by a well of something. Emotion? Whatever the hell it was, he wasn't sure he liked it. "You did that for me?"

"Well, yeah," she laughed. "It's my job." She tucked a lock of hair behind her ear. "And as a bonus, they want *you*. Not the Coulter name. It's sort of a detriment. To them *Coulter* is stodgy, old guard. But Dax? Dax is new school."

"You managed to do something my agent couldn't."

"It's no big deal, Dax. It's my—"

His brain stuttered. She was saying something about Dax Coulter... His senses were flooded with her, and her scent and her lips and her hair. The only way to make the roaring stop was to let himself drown.

TWELVE

Danger, Will Robinson! Danger! Asha couldn't move. Dax's hooded gaze was trained on her lips, and for the life of her, she couldn't think. She liked him looking at her like that. Like he could eat her up in one swallow and still want more. Heat radiated from his body, enveloping her, soothing and coaxing through nothing but proximity.

She had a plan. She *loved* plans. Too bad her body had a whole other, *unintended* plan. She felt like one giant raw nerve. She'd seriously done more talking than she'd planned. The good news was he'd opened up. Mission accomplished. The bad news was, she'd opened up, too, and now she was vulnerable.

Her name was a whispered caress, and when she tipped her head up to meet his gaze, his lips brushed over hers.

The first kiss was tentative, a whispered question. He drew back a little, waiting, asking.

A shiver ran through her, and she had no choice but to chase his kiss with one of her own, twining their fingers together as she did. His free hand came up to cup the back of her head, his fingers aligning with the bones on the back of her neck before slipping down under the collar of her blouse.

His kisses missed their mark, landing on the corner of her mouth and cheek, while his fingers traced the skin beneath her satin collar, moving along the seam toward the front of her blouse, where the buttons began just below the hollow at the base of her throat.

She couldn't breathe. She couldn't slow her heart rate. She couldn't think. In those moments, all she knew was him. His touch. His mouth.

Dax's finger hovered at the top button, waiting.

She let go of his other hand and reached for the loose fabric of his shirt where it was tucked into his pants, tugging it free. Dax eagerly unbuttoned her blouse, pausing so she could pull his shirt up and over his head before she shrugged out of her own.

She pulled him with her onto the bed, lying back while he buried his face in her chest. He reached up and pulled aside the silky fabric of her bra. Cupping her breasts in his warm hands, he moaned. Her breath hitched. *Oh, God. Oh, God.* Need pulled at her core. Her skin tingled and every synapse in her brain fired. Holy hell. Was this what she'd been missing out on?

Her hands traced the lines of muscle along his arms and abdomen, pressing lightly into his skin like a sculptor molding clay. She drew one of them slowly down Dax's arm to the hand cupping her breast and pressed it firmer to her. *Yes. That felt so damn—* His thumb teased her nipple, raising it to a peak. *Holy shit.* She rocked her hips into his, seeking...

She arched toward him, and his hand slipped to her back, first unhooking her bra, then trying to find a way down the back of her skirt. She laughed as the high waist of the skirt proved to be too difficult an obstacle for Dax to manage one-handed. Her laughter stopped abruptly when he bent his head to kiss her again, and ran that hand over the curve of her buttock, using it to pull her tight against him to feel the full extent of his arousal. *Oh, wow.*

She reached for Dax's hand once more, tugging it away from her ass and guiding it to the hem of her skirt. He shifted his weight and moved his body down hers, leaving a trail of kisses along her neck, clavicle, and breasts, and over her stomach just where the lightly tanned skin disappeared beneath the tightly woven grey cotton of her pencil skirt.

Her heart hammered as he discarded her bra. Dax's hands slid up her calves to massage the soft spot at the back of her knee. Hell. She wanted to open her legs to him but the skirt had no give. Before she could reach down to hike the constrictive fabric out of the way herself, his hand slid up the back of her thigh, pushing the skirt up and out of his path. *More.* Hell, she needed more.

"God...taste so good...soft...I can't..." Dax whispered against her skin as he kissed, sucked, licked. He covered her nipple completely with his lips, his warm breath a tease and caress all in one.

When he retreated and then leaned in again, she held her breath. *Oh, God.* "Dax. Ple—"

Her name was a whisper on his lips, before he laved her nipple and sucked her deep. With a moan, Asha arched her back and slid her hands into his hair. She tugged him close as he pulled deep. There was something she was supposed to remember. Some line she was supposed to think about. But all that mattered to her in this moment, in his arms, was how she felt. How he could make her feel.

Dax rocked his hips into her, the rigid length of him pressing into her, making her so slick, so, so hot.

With a frustrated growl, he released her, turned her to her side, yanked down her zipper, and then tugged off her skirt. When he turned her back over, his eyes burned. The dim light of the room made his beautiful features seem more pronounced. "You are so beautiful."

His soft words were punctuated with a tender kiss. One that quickly morphed into a flaming wildfire. He was going to burn her up with his touch alone, and she wouldn't survive it. But like a moth to a flame, she craved his heat. She wanted the promised incineration.

His hand traced over her breast and his eyes locked on hers as it swept over her belly. When he teased his finger at the juncture of her thighs, just under the elastic of her panties, she clung to him as if her hips took on a life of their own, begging for his touch. Begging him to touch her where she needed. He teased the elastic gently, before slipping underneath, and running his finger over her smooth skin.

He dropped his forehead to hers. "You are so fucking wet. All I want to do is bury myself right here." His finger pressed into her, oh-so-gently, and she stiffened.

"Oh, my God, Dax."

"Shh, it's okay. I'm not going to hurt you. Tell me what you like. I just want to make you feel good..." He stroked his finger over her slit then gently teased her clit. He licked his bottom lip then whispered, "So, so good. Show me, Asha. How do I do that?"

She reached for that clawing desire, the need that'd had her body humming for the last couple of weeks, but the more she reached for it, the more it eluded her. She didn't know what to tell him. "Dax, I—"

He kissed the hollow just behind her ear as he circled the sensitive bundle of nerves with his finger and she lost all brain function. "Help me, sweetheart. Teach me what you like."

"I—" Oh God, she needed him to keep going. To *not* stop. To *never* stop. "I—I don't know. I've never done this before."

The moment the words were out of her mouth, she froze.

Oh, shit. What had she just said? *Out loud.* To Dax-I'm-a-freaking-sex-God-Coulter?

Dax raised his head slowly to meet her gaze. Even as his fingers stroked over her clit, his eyes searched hers for truth.

When he saw it, he frowned. But he didn't release her. "You're a virgin." He said it as more statement than question.

She opened her mouth. Closed it. *Once more with feeling.* "Y-yes."

It was only then that she saw it. The flash of something. Not anger, more like pain. Then he gritted his teeth and gently removed his finger as he dropped his forehead to hers. "Fuck. I am so goddamned sorry."

She missed his heat as soon as he was gone. But not just his touch, the reverent way he'd looked at her. He covered her up with the sheet and scooted to the edge of the bed.

Aching for his touch, Asha propped herself up on her elbows.

He gave her his back from where he sat, hunched at the foot of the bed, his head bowed.

"Dax?" she breathed, suddenly very aware of her half-naked state, and how cool the temperature in the room really was. She scrambled to her knees and crawled to him.

"I shouldn't have done that. I'm really fucking sorry. I'm such an asshole."

A wash of shame and guilt spilled over her. But a stronger flash of rebellion overpowered it. "Why?" It was technically a question, but she meant it to be rhetorical, a challenge. She reached out and caressed the knot of muscle where his neck branched out to his shoulders. He tensed briefly, before finally relaxing.

"I am a dick. Everyone knows this. *I* know it. And I didn't think it was possible, but I've actually made it worse. I promised your brother I would look out for you. Not—" he muttered "—*this*."

She blinked. "You stopped because you promised my brother?"

Dax's head shot up as he registered the anger in her voice. She shoved her arms into the sleeves of her shirt, but her hands shook too much to button it properly. She could only hold it closed while she turned on Dax.

"You don't think we should sleep together because *my brother* might object? Are you saying *my brother* gets to determine who I sleep with, and when?"

"What?" Dax asked, completely thrown by the track her mind had taken. "No!" He jumped to his feet and moved toward her. "You're a virgin. And this, what I almost just did, is typical Dax. I might not know shit, but I do know your first time should matter."

"Shouldn't I say how it goes?"

He licked his lips and her gaze fixated on his tongue. "Absolutely. But I get to be a good guy for once. Please let me."

The tears pricked behind her eyes, but she blinked them away. This was fine. Whatever. So what, if she just got rejected by the guy who'd fuck anything that moved. "It's fine. We'll forget it happened."

"Asha. This has nothing to do—"

She couldn't take it if he kept apologizing. "It's fine. A momentary lapse in judgment."

His brows snapped down. "Are you serious, right now?"

"Yep. Whole thing forgotten. We got carried away."

His frown only deepened. "That's how you want to play it?"

She nodded. "Dax, I'm already embarrassed and mortified enough. Can you just let it go?"

He searched her gaze intently before grabbing his discarded shirt. "Asha—"

"I'm okay. Give me the night, and it's back to normal."

She managed to hold it together until he finally left. She knew one thing. Okay, two. Kissing Dax and getting intimate with him had ruined her for other guys. Fact. Second, there was no way they could ever be alone together again. Ever.

"Sam, I did something stupid." Asha sat against the hotel room door, with a blanket wrapped around her.

"Well considering my bestie is no dummy, there must have been extenuating circumstances. Are we talking rule number one, two, three, or four?"

Asha's rules were simple.

1. Do not screw up at work
2. Do not under any circumstances sleep with one of the players
3. Do not under any circumstances fall in love with one of the players.
4. Do not let a relationship interfere with her job.

"This is in more rule two territory."

Sam was her best friend. Hell, sometimes it felt like her only friend. They'd known each other since they were three. And Sam hadn't abandoned her through those awkward teen years, or even when she had been shipped off to college at fifteen and a half. "I beg to differ. That Asha apparently has left the building and has been replaced with a hormonal, irrational one."

There was a beat of silence. Then Sam said. "Asha baby, are you telling me you finally lost your V card?"

"No." She could most feel the sigh. "But, that was not for lack of trying."

"I don't understand. Start at the beginning and leave nothing out. I want to know everything about the hot piece of man that got Asha Wix to sit up and take notice."

Asha rambled out the story, leaving out the TMI parts, even though Sam begged for them.

"Dude, you were seriously about to break rule number two."

"I know, Sam. I know. It was so stupid. And the moment he kissed me, it was like I wasn't even listening to the rational part of my brain that screamed, 'Hey, what are you thinking?'"

"Uh, baby girl, I just looked him up. That is Dax-fucking-Coulter? You've been holding out. And if you don't jump him, I will. I mean the guy looks like Superman, but leaner. Do you see the abs on him?"

"Yes—no. I don't know. Look, what do I do?"

"Well, what do you want to do?

"I don't want to think with my—"

"Vajayjay," Sam offered helpfully.

"Sam, I'm serious."

"Okay, okay." Her best friend laughed. "I get it. But, honey, all your life, you've been Asha Wix. You are the perfect student, the perfect daughter, the perfect sister. You have never stepped a toe out of line. You have to remember, though, that no one is truly perfect, and I think you should take your own advice to Mr. Rock-Me-in-the-Sack, and not beat yourself up over it. You and I both know there would be a real connection there, otherwise you wouldn't have been trying to see if he really is a sex god."

"He's not—"

"What? A sex god?"

Asha flushed. "No, I mean, he's obviously good looking and sexy. But that profile that you see of him...that's not him. *He* stopped. I wanted to, but *he* pulled back, trying to be respectful."

"And honey, that's great. I just don't want you to get in too deep here. As long as he's lovely to you, then great. Hook up all you want. But, don't get attached. He's a professional athlete. He's a player in more ways than one. And you certainly don't fall in love with a guy like that."

"I know." Asha ran a hand through her hair. "I need to get over this. Back to business."

Sam's exhale was long, and not so quiet. "That's not what I'm saying. I think you spend so much time being perfect you could use some fun. I'm just asking you not to fall for this guy. You've waited a long time to have some guy rev you up like that. It's good for you. Remember what your mom always used to fight with your Dad about. How she wanted you guys to live a full life. This is what she meant. Fun is part of that."

"I hear you Sam, but this is my career. What happened... I can't let it happen again. It's too important."

"You're not going to listen to me, are you?" Sam asked.

"Normally, I would. You are all-knowing. But I've worked so hard. And you're right, Dax Coulter isn't a sticker. I just have to keep my distance."

Sam only laughed wryly. "Yeah, good luck with that."

STUMBLING THROUGH HIS DOOR, DAX CROSSED THE ROOM and flopped facedown on the bed, breathing in the scent of the cheap detergent the hotel used to launder the sheets. He set his alarm for eight-thirty, and then headed to take a shower. As reluctant as he was to wash the scent of Asha from his skin, he wouldn't be able to sleep with it there, and he knew he should at least try to get some rest.

The water pressure was high, and it beat down on all the

sore places, as well as muscles that would be worse in a few hours. He fought to push the thoughts of Asha from his head.

It never happened, he repeated to himself. *For all intents and purposes, it never happened. Think of what would happen if it got out—do you really want to hurt her career like that? Do you want that hanging over your head? And she may not care what Damon thinks—and she does have a point—but it would still change things between you and Damon. He wouldn't be able to look at you without thinking of the things you've done with his sister.*

He clung to those thoughts, and waited for the guilt to bloom in his chest at the thought of his betrayal, but it didn't happen. He knew that what happened between him and Asha would never—*could never*—happen again, and for that reason he was incapable of regret.

As the sad reality of that concept sunk in, a chill ran through him, as though the water from the shower had suddenly gone cold. He turned it up hotter, and a part of him knew he was in danger of scalding his skin, but he couldn't register the heat.

He turned the water off, toweled down, and headed to bed, certain of finding bliss—whether in the oblivion of sleep or in dreams of Asha.

THIRTEEN

Forgetting Asha and what had happened in her room was next to impossible for Dax. Hell, the only time he wasn't thinking of her or what she tasted like, was when he was on the field. And lucky for them, they had been winning.

The team headed back to Jacksonville for three days before hitting the road again for Denver. The players' curfew remained the same, but with the elevation, most of the guys were less inclined to take advantage of the nightlife Denver had to offer and more inclined to acclimatize.

And while things on the field were looking good, he couldn't take his eyes off of Asha. All it took to get him going was hearing her laugh. When he and Asha were out for dinner with a few other players and their PR buddies, he had to snap his attention away any time she looked at him. While he was having a problem with focus, she seemed...completely unaffected. As if what had happened with them had zero effect on her.

"I don't know what you've done, but you seem to have Coulter well under control," Aaron Espenson commented from across the table. "He's been more...subdued the last week."

"Let's hope it lasts," Asha laughed.

Dax knew it was standard ribbing, but he hated it coming from her.

"So, how'd your pitch go?"

Dax glared at Espenson. He needed to shut up, for starters. Then maybe stop looking at Asha like she was a steak and he was starving.

Asha flinched. "Well...I got some pushback, but I was expecting that."

Aaron looked skeptical. "I was in there when they were looking over the chatter for Coulter these last few weeks, and they were pleased."

"We'll see if they're still pleased in a month or two." Asha said cautiously and slid a glance at Dax again. He wasn't looking away this time. From where he sat, he could see her pupils dilate when her lips parted. Blood roared in his skull, and he couldn't hear a thing. Fuck, she was so beautiful. But she flushed and broke eye contact.

Okay, so maybe he wasn't the only one affected.

Phil Clark, who'd been eavesdropping on their conversation asked, "What *was* your pitch anyway? I went in after you did, and they looked like they'd just found out someone they loved was being held hostage."

"They did look a little green," she grinned. She enjoyed holding management by the balls. If possible, it made Dax feel even more attracted to her. "I think they're relying too heavily on Dax's last name."

"But he's a Coulter," Aaron interrupted, stating the obvious.

"Yeah, but if they play that up, they're putting a very specific kind of pressure on him. And he doesn't have to be Rory Coulter. He can be Dax and be great. The focus belongs on him. And we can make him shine." Dax kept his eyes down. She was fighting *for* him. No one *ever* fought for him. She continued, "He is never going to *be* a player like his grandfather, because the game isn't the same as it was back then. I think he has incredible potential, *if* we give him the room to figure it out for himself."

"No wonder they looked baffled," Phil muttered. "You're supposed to be the most promising of the new hires, and you walked in there to shoot down the easiest marketing plan they had."

"It just sounds to me like *you* missed a few classes of Marketing 101." Aaron's tone was patronizing.

Dax just barely resisted the urge to walk over to the other side of the table and hit the guy.

But Asha didn't need him. "In my experience marketing *people* is about more than just the customer." Her voice was clear. "If the player isn't happy, it doesn't matter how much you push an angle. It won't ring true and the fans will not only pick up on the disparity, it can affect their view of the organization as a whole."

"If you think ignoring his lineage is going to—"

"I'm not saying ignore it altogether, I'm saying let someone else bring it up first," she interrupted, causing both Phil and Aaron to draw back in surprise. "If we bring it up and shove it in the media's faces, we come off looking like his name is the only reason he's here. Which, if you've seen him run a pass, is completely inaccurate."

"I wouldn't be surprised if they let you have your way just to shut you up," Phil remarked under his breath.

Asha narrowed her gaze and Dax knew where this was going. Someone was getting an ass-handing. He excused himself and headed for her end of the table. "Hey, Asha, can we go over the notes for the endorser pitch?"

With a steely-eyed glance, she looked like she wanted to argue, but then she nodded. "Sure, let's go."

As they walked out, he kept his voice low. "You okay?"

"You didn't have to save me."

"Are you kidding me? I knew you were going to rip him a new one."

The autumn evening chill combined with the thinner air made her shiver. Dax fell into step beside her, staying close to try and cut some of the wind, until they passed a café.

"D'you mind if we pop in here, real quick?" he asked.

Asha shrugged. "Whatever."

Maybe chocolate would help calm her. Women loved chocolate, right? Being around her, he felt like he knew nothing about women.

After retrieving a few dessert options from the counter, Dax set up camp at a table along the wall, where they could see people pass on the sidewalk but weren't shoved up against the glass to be watched in turn. The minute they were settled, Dax dove into a large piece of chocolate cake.

"I should know better by now," Asha said as she watched him, "but you don't seem to be as strict with your nutrition as some of the other players."

He laughed as he chewed and swallowed. "I tried it for a while once in college, but I was miserable and I couldn't see that it really improved my performance enough to justify how grumpy it made me. Actually, Damon was the one who told me to just eat what the fuck I wanted and stop chewing everyone out instead."

Asha laughed and nodded, filling her mouth with a bite of brownie coated with a thick layer of mint icing. She sighed and closed her eyes. And he couldn't take his eyes off of her. *Focus, dude.*

"From what I saw earlier, you don't always like to do what people expect either," he said.

She rolled her eyes. "My job isn't to do what people expect, but to do my job the best way I see fit. If that means I surprise them, it's on them for being narrow-minded in the first place. Honestly, my ability to think outside the box was supposed to be one of the reasons why they hired me. Now I'm being criticized for it. Sorry," she apologized. "I shouldn't have gone off like that." She took another huge bite of her brownie and chewed quietly for a moment.

"Don't worry about it," Dax said as he continued devouring his piece of chocolate cake. She'd done it for him. "You've got more nerve than most of those assholes. They've gotten too used to things being a certain way, and it's made them lazy. The whole point of the shakeup was to change things, because the old ways weren't working. Look at the team now. We've finally been playing well."

"So do the new coaches have you guys running through a lot of the old plays, or have they got you trying different things?" she asked once her mouth was empty.

He shrugged. "Bit of both. Can't fall into predictability, or it makes it easier for your opponents to adjust their play to stop you."

"Have you ever designed a play yourself?"

Dax took another bite of cake, and after a moment, shook his head. No, he hadn't. But it didn't mean he didn't want to. Sometimes he could see the openings in ways the QB couldn't.

"So, no. Have you ever *tried* to design a play before?" she said, pushing the issue.

"It's not my place to suggest plays," he answered. "I'm a wide receiver. I have to go where I'm told, when I'm told, and do what I can to catch the ball. QB calls the plays, and I execute them."

"So basically, you're saying you haven't because it isn't your job?" She unfolded a napkin, and took a highlighter from her purse. "Explain to me one of your favorite plays," she prompted.

Man, she didn't give up.

She really wanted to know? He narrowed his eyes at her,

skeptical and uncertain, but set his fork down, took the marker from her, and drew a series of Xs, Os, and arrows, narrating the different positions and the responsibilities of those players.

When he was finished, Asha asked him a series of questions about how they might adjust on the field if the opposing team reacted in this way instead of that. He sometimes forgot that she knew the game so well. Her father was the commissioner of the NFL, for the love of God. She'd better know the game. He examined the diagram on the napkin, and turned it slightly so he could picture the larger field of play. All the while aware of Asha's gaze on him.

When she'd run out of questions regarding the first play, she asked him to illuminate the details of a second. As she talked, she helped him finish his cake. After enjoying the last few bites, Dax grabbed another napkin and did the same as before while Asha finished her brownie. His enthusiasm grew, but he kept a tight hold on it. He liked doing this stuff, but he couldn't let himself get too carried away.

She glanced at her watch, and Dax groaned quietly. Seriously, this curfew was cramping his style. He wanted more alone time with her.

"We should head back to the hotel now," she said as she stood and tossed her trash. Dax crumpled the napkins along with his own trash, and returned the marker.

They were back on the sidewalk when his curiosity got the best of him.

"Asha... Are we...okay?" Dumbass. "Jeez, I sound..."

She interrupted, and darted a glance around them. "I thought we weren't talking about it. Or *thinking* about it." She tugged on her watch.

"*You* said we weren't thinking about it. I've done a lot of... thinking." Sure, that's what he called that dance with his cock every night.

"Dax, please."

"Okay, fine." he sighed, changing the subject. "Why'd you ask about those plays in there?"

"Why not? I think that understanding as much as I can about something helps me to market it better. Now I know more about what your specific role is on the field," she said evasively.

Dax didn't say anything else, but he did watch her closely as they walked into the lobby. She knew his position inside and out. She was Damon's sister, after all. But just like that talk she didn't want to have, he'd leave it alone for now.

FOURTEEN

It was a close game—14-13—but the team won against Denver. Another game in which a last-minute field goal made the difference. But this time, the field goal was theirs. It was only their third win of the season, and they still had a long way to go, but the atmosphere around the team was changing. Even coach was happy. And Dax had *never* seen that dude happy since he'd joined the team.

Not only had the team played their best, Dax had one of his best games—and that meant the press wanted to speak with him. And that meant game talk. *Coulter* game talk.

Asha was waiting for him outside the pressroom. She was actually vibrating with energy. He couldn't help his automatic smile. He had to cool it, or someone would figure it out that he was just a little obsessed with seeing her smile.

Play it cool.

"Good job today. I mingled with the press a bit to get a feel for the questions they wanted to ask, and to guide them in the direction we want," she said quickly, before giving him a brief list of vetted reporters to call on. "Keep your answers short and to the point. Smile, but try to keep it modest. If you're asked about your family's reaction or opinions..."

"I'll do what I usually do—tell them to ask them themselves," Dax finished.

She frowned. "What? No. That comes off as resentful or dismissive." Asha huffed out a short breath, and then reached out to pick lint off his shirt. "Tell them that while you don't speak for your family as a whole, *you* are pleased with what you've managed to accomplish today, and *you* hope there will be more games like this one. Don't try to disregard the reporters' questions, but try to reframe your answers so that the focus is on *you* and *your* role with this team. The team is what you're focused on, and when it comes to your performance, they're the ones whose opinion matters to you first. Okay?"

"I think so," he said with a nod.

She reached up and took hold of him by the shoulders, and for a half-second he thought she might rise up on her toes to give him a kiss. His heart pounded, and the blood rushed in his skull. He *wanted* her to kiss him, wanted the press of her soft, full lips on his. Instead, she looked him square in the eye like she was looking for something, then released him with a quiet, "Good luck."

The wave of disappointment hit hard. "Thanks."

It was certainly easier to be polite and agreeable with the reporters after having such a good game. He resisted the bait a few of them threw his way without entirely losing his charm. He even managed to get some good banter going with one of the reporters. For the first time, he walked out of the room confident about his performance—on and *off* the field.

Some of the guys had plans to head out after the game to celebrate. Problem was, he knew that if he went, Asha would wind up tagging along, too. Which meant they'd have an audience. And everyone would know he had a problem. But at the same time, it also meant more time with her. And depending on where the guys wanted to go, more time with her was a very appealing prospect.

"Really?" she said with a frown, when he offered the invitation.

"It'll be better than the other night, I promise," Dax told her. Then he winced, when he thought back to the night he'd kissed her...like a moron.

"Oh, after that interview, I think I can trust Phil and Aaron to keep their criticisms to themselves," she said firmly. "I just...I liked it better at the café. I'm better one-on-one. But another dinner out will be fine. Everyone going back to the hotel to change first?"

"Yeah. But I think dinner and a lounge spot. We'll meet up in the lobby and head out together. Seven o'clock?"

"All right. I'll see you then."

Just one problem—how was he going to keep his hands off of her tonight?

DAX WAS ONE OF THE FIRST OF HIS TEAMMATES TO MAKE IT to the lobby. He flopped into a chair to wait, and pulled out his cell phone to finally check the messages from his family.

They pretty much followed their standard scripts from the previous weeks' games, but Dax could detect an uptick in the sincerity. None of them even felt the need to mention the fast-approaching wedding. For once, they were all focused on him in a way that was genuinely complimentary. Except Gage. Of course, that was more of the same. But for some reason, his father hadn't called personally. Instead, Echo had conveyed his congratulations, along with her own message to him.

She had probably caught the game at their parents' house

with their father—and Gramps—sitting across the room from her when she'd called. They'd done it before, but never when Dax had played as well as he had that day.

In fact, the longer he thought about it, the more unusual it felt. There were plenty of times when Echo had watched the game with their parents that Dad had still gone out of his way to leave him a message of his own. And something in his sister's tone was...off.

"Hey, man." Samuels plopped into the seat next to Dax, and immediately began complimenting Dax on his numbers for the game, dragging Dax out of his reverie. Dax forced himself to focus. Maybe he'd call home a little later and check on his Dad.

"Caught some of your post-game interview on the TV upstairs, too. Looked pretty good, man. Don't know which you handled better today, the ball or the press."

"Thanks," he muttered.

"So now my question to you is, are you being adequately *handled* between games? Is that why you've been so on-point lately?" Samuels waggled his eyebrows suggestively, and a chill ran down Dax's spine.

This is what she meant. What she'd been warned about. "Asha? She's not my type. You know how I like my girls. Available. Have you seen Damon Wix? I am not messing with his sister. Besides, she's my babysitter. We all got one." He said it in an effort to brush the accusation off and move on to a new subject. "Yours is sitting right over there," he said with a nod.

Samuels tensed as he glanced over his shoulder to see Aaron Espenson hovering by the elevator, waiting for the rest of their party to reach the ground floor. He was a new hire like Asha, but more nervous about being around the players. Probably because most of them could snap him like a twig. And after the way Dax caught him looking at Asha, he was not a fan.

"Guy's like a mosquito that won't leave ya alone," Samuels

assessed with an eye roll and a shake of the head. "Now, *your* shadow...her, I could get used to. Seems like you have."

"Uh-uh," Dax said, shaking his head. "Wix, remember? I like my head where it is. I'm not going there."

"Well, *if* you haven't, you should get on it. Fuck Wix. We'd back you. Besides, everyone thinks you are, anyway," Samuels shrugged.

Shit. Shit. Shit. *Be cool.*

"What? Why would anyone think that?" Dax hoped the quiet, desperate storm inside remained hidden.

"'Cause she's hot, and you're clearly into her," Johnson said from behind the pair of them. He had moved silently across the lobby to lean over them, with one hand on the back of each of their chairs. "Something about that stick-up-the-ass attitude that makes a dude want to give her some stick. Know what I mean?"

Samuels jumped in his seat before reaching back to give Johnson a smack, muttering, "Son of a bitch," under his breath.

Dax searched for words, but between the surprise of Johnson's undetected appearance and his own struggle to find a way of believably denying his interest in Asha, he was at a loss. *It never happened. She's off limits*, his internal mantra resurfaced.

"Why else would you take off after her like that at the restaurant the other day?" Samuels asked.

"I did that to keep her from ripping homeboy a new one. Have you ever seen her angry? All big words and chilly tone. It'll give any guy a limp dick." He shrugged. "I'm not going there. Besides, you think I'm gonna take this pretty mug off the market?"

"Guess that's a valid excuse for it," Samuels admitted. "You do like the pussy. Wondered how you were gonna get past the curfew thing."

Dax ground his teeth, but forced a grin. "I manage."

"Doesn't mean you can't be into her, though," Johnson

pointed out, straightening up and shooting Dax a mischievous grin.

Dax turned back to look over his shoulder at Johnson, but the opening elevator caught his attention. Asha stepped out in a form-hugging dress like the fuchsia one she'd worn to the club a few weeks ago, but this one was emerald green. She'd done something different with her hair as well, pulling it up into a loose pile on top of her head instead of leaving it loose around her shoulders. *Holy fuck.*

Dax was vaguely aware of the laughter coming from his two teammates, and knew that he'd never hear the end of their teasing now. He also didn't give a shit. If they thought he had an interest in her, it would keep the rest of them from hitting on her themselves—or making other crude comments at her expense.

But with that thought came an unwanted flood of jealousy. None of these fuckers had better go near her. There was generally a team code, but the way she looked, there was a chance that someone might forget.

He wasn't the only one whose attention had perked up at Asha's entrance. The hovering Aaron swooped in and walked alongside her as she crossed the lobby to meet Dax and the other players. To Dax's silent delight, Asha didn't look too pleased about it and came to stand next to him. Aaron glowered but backed off.

"How many more are we waiting for?" she asked the group at large.

"Just three," Samuels said, eyeing Dax when Asha's attention turned elsewhere.

Dax ignored him. It was going to be a long night. When the coast was clear, she glared at him.

"What's going on?" she muttered under her breath. "Why are the guys acting weird?"

"Don't worry about it."

Later at dinner, he watched her from down the table again, and he noted the way Aaron paid all his attention to her. Okay, he might have been watching a little too closely. Several times, Samuels had to poke him to get his attention.

Like he gave a shit. He wanted to make sure Aaron didn't touch her. *Or what, asshole? She's not yours.* Fuck. Hey, even if she was technically off-limits, thinking about her wasn't.

When Aaron's hand snuck below the edge of the table and he leaned into her, Dax's fingers curled tightly around the handle of his steak knife. He couldn't see what the shit was actually up to, but he could imagine how close to Asha's bare thigh he was, as the hem of that rich, green dress rode up whenever she sat down.

He remembered how soft her skin was just there, and the way it slid against his thigh as he had rocked against her. He remembered how she'd moaned his name.

Dax looked away and struggled to focus. He had to. Or everyone would easily guess the path of his thoughts. *Murder.* Absolute murder.

Every now and again, he caught her glancing at him and realized he'd been staring. He forced himself to look away from her for the rest of the meal. *Mostly.*

Some of the guys wanted to try and find a club after they hit up the lounge, but since they would be on a plane bright and early, the PR contingent was able to successfully encourage an early return to the hotel.

They all piled into the elevator, and Dax just tried to keep his head above water and not stare at her. If he moved, he'd be touching her. And, he'd done really well tonight. *Bullshit.* Okay, most nights he did well. Sure, his little habit with her and the constant, incessant dreams about how she would taste and how it would feel to slide into her warm, velvet embrace kept him up more nights than he cared to think about. And yeah, okay, the little habit of jerking off to the memory of her soft lips was...a problem.

But he hadn't actually touched her...so that was a win, right?

The guys in the elevator talked amongst themselves until the doors opened, and some women from a bachelorette party climbed in, making the elevator feel like a tin of sardines.

Of course, his teammates couldn't help themselves, shamelessly flirting with the group of women who, naturally, flirted back. Dax tried to keep his eyes on the moving numbers. And in an effort to keep from inhaling Asha's sweet scent, he held his breath. Just another few seconds and he'd be free. Just one more second.

The lights flickered, and everybody froze. Asha's shoulders went still, and Dax watched her stiff body language as she ignored Aaron whispering something in her ear. Dax forced his fists to unfurl. The guy found her attractive. It wasn't like Dax could fault his taste. But every male instinct screamed *mine*. Which was ridiculous.

So they'd made out...*once*. He'd done dirtier things than that when he was in junior high school. But it was different with her, and more than the fact that she was forbidden. He'd dated lots of girls who weren't supposed to have a boyfriend, or who had boyfriends and wanted a walk on the wild side. Forbidden wasn't the pull.

It was her. Her taste, her lips. Fuck, he had to breathe. Her goddamn scent.

The lights flickered again, and this time everything went dark. Predictably, everyone reached for something to steady themselves.

Someone in the bachelorette party squealed. Samuels and Ellis offered their bodies as something firm to hold on to. And then he heard Samuels say, "I swear to God, Ellis, that better not be your hand on my ass."

And Asha, well, she'd stumbled right back into him. Her fine ass currently cradled his dick. *Oh, fuck.* Instinctively, he snapped his hands to her waist to steady her, and she rewarded him with a little wiggle. *Shit. Shit. Fucking hell. Shit. Not good. Not okay. Not—*

He needed to let go of her. He should—*except*, he didn't. Instead, his hand smoothed over her waist to the flat expanse of her belly, and tucked her even closer. The loud chatter in the elevator was enough to mask her soft sigh. But he could feel it.

Next to her, the pencil pusher asked, "Ash, are you okay?"

Dax widened his hand and kept pressing her into him. The little rocking motions of her hips were going to fucking cripple him.

With a shaky voice, she replied. "Uh...y-yes."

"Do you need to hold on to me?" Aaron asked. Dax was really going to kill the little shit. Asha was *his*.

"N-no. I'm, uh, on solid ground."

"Are you sure? You sound funny."

Dax leaned down to her ear. In her towering heels, he didn't have far to go. He didn't say anything, just let his warm breath tickle her ear. So she would know who was touching her. Know whose cock lay nestled between the globes of her ass.

This is stupid. Reckless... Damn hot.

"I'm fine, Aaron." Her voice was tight, hoarse. "Just not a fan of not seeing what's happening."

Yeah, that makes two of us, sweetheart. Dax would kill to see the look on her face right now. To watch her pupils dilate. To see how much he was turning her on. She grabbed on to his leg to steady herself, even as he bent his knees slightly to give himself a better— Oh, yeah. So good.

His brain offered him the beautiful mental image of him sliding into her like this, as she maybe held onto the wall. His cock throbbed. But it wasn't until her delicate hand slid between them to stroke him through his slacks that Dax muttered a low, "Fuck."

Samuels, ever helpful, laughed and said, "What's the matter, Coulter, afraid of the dark?"

She palmed him gently, and his eyes crossed as he tried to force his brain to work. *Come on, you shitty piece of gray matter. Stop this train.* Except he didn't want to get off...the train, that was. Getting off with Asha, now that was something he was all over right now.

"Fuck you, Samuels."

He knew his breathing was ragged, and if he wasn't careful, someone was going to realize what they were doing to each other. But right about now, he could give a fuck. All he wanted was *more* of her touch. *More* of her hands. He wanted her soft skin, her lips, her—

The low buzz of electricity was his only warning. But he knew what it meant.

Gently, he set her away from him and removed her hand from his pulsing erection, then forced himself to lean back against the wall. Three, two, one and...on came the lights.

Ellis and one of the bridesmaids were all over each other, but jumped quickly apart. Yeah, he wasn't the only one who had that idea.

When the elevator chimed again and started to move, he released the breath he'd been holding. Everyone jumped off on Asha's floor. Probably safer to take the stairs for the time being.

Dax wanted to walk Asha back to her room like he had the last time, but with Aaron standing beside her, he was forced to follow his teammates.

"You up for a session in the exercise room?" Samuels asked.

"Yeah," Johnson agreed. "Gonna ride this high as long as it lasts. I'm sure Mills'll be riding us hard at practice the next few days to make sure we don't let it all go to our heads. You comin', Coulter?"

"I think I'm gonna call it a night, actually," he muttered as he pulled his keycard from his pocket. "I've gotta call my folks back."

He knew it was a flimsy excuse, and the gesture he caught Samuels making at Johnson made him scowl. Safely in his room, he closed and locked the door behind him, leaned against it, and tried not to think of Asha. Or what Aaron was trying to *do* with Asha.

FIFTEEN

Asha closed the door to her room and locked it, being sure to draw the bolt as well. She listened for Aaron's steps to disappear down the hall before letting out the breath she'd been holding. She slipped off her heels and moaned as she sunk her feet into the plush carpet. Pulling out her loose and comfortable pajamas, she repeatedly told herself, *It could have been worse— Phil could have joined us.*

Once she was ready for bed, her mind drifted to her favorite off limits subject. *Dax.* He'd been watching her. A lot. She could *feel* the heat of his gaze on her. Every time she moved. Every time she breathed. And it made her weak. Too breathy, too...*needy.*

She wasn't an idiot, and she realized his teammates were starting to notice. Her coworkers were starting to notice. Except Aaron. *He* somehow got it in his head that she would be interested in him. She wasn't interested in anyone. Dax didn't count. He wasn't a possibility.

She had to talk to him about it before the gossip got out of hand. The last thing they needed was for someone like Aaron to get wind of the idea and use it against her. He was just that slimy.

The interviews Dax had done after the day's game had gone really well, but her bosses were still skeptical about her angle for handling his presentation to the media and the fans. There were too many things they had to gain by firing her at the first excuse that presented itself.

She had to tell Dax to cool it, even if it meant they had to limit their professional interactions to the phone. The more they hung out, the more she wanted to hang with him. *Pathetic.* She knew it. She was officially a groupie; a *proho*, just without the '*ho*' part. The way the team was improving, some of the tighter restrictions might be loosened after their next home game. She had a feeling that would be the deciding factor.

She crawled onto the bed and leaned back into the pillows as she dialed Dax's cell. It rang twice before he answered, breathing heavily.

"Perfect fucking timing," he growled.

"Sorry, I thought you preferred to hit the exercise room in the morning," she apologized.

"I do," he groaned. And something dark and needy pulled low in her body.

"Then why do you sound so out of breath?" Her skin heated when her mind offered several helpful scenarios for his condition. All of them had to do with him being...naked.

His breathing was ragged. "Asha. Don't ask me that... Please."

The pulsing between her legs increased, and she bit her lip. She didn't want to know. But at the same time, she did. "Dax, what are you doing?"

"I'm wondering what would have happened if I'd walked you to your room tonight."

Her breath caught. "Dax..."

His voice had gone low, guttural. "Don't tell me you never touch yourself when you think of...someone."

"N—no—I—"

"Sounds like you're blushing." Of course, she was. He continued. "Anybody I know, Asha?"

"You agreed," she reminded him.

"No. You promised, and we're each in our own rooms, completely alone. This is just talk. That's all. A fantasy," he pointed out. "I can't lay a finger on you. But...if I could...I'd start by sliding my hand up your thigh, and hiking that skirt of yours up and out of the way."

"No, you wouldn't." She couldn't keep the smile out of her voice. "Because I've already changed out of that dress."

His voice dropped an octave. "You're already naked? Excellent. In that case—"

"I'm in pajamas, jackass," she laughed.

"Well, then, I'll just have to take them off you, won't I?" he whispered. "Why is the thought of you in flannel pajamas so hot?"

"And who said anything about flannel?" She smirked.

There was a pause. "You're killing me. I wanted to touch you so bad on the elevator tonight. I swear to God, I wanted to hike up your dress and see if you wanted me as much as I want you. I *still* want to see how wet you are."

The pulsing was more insistent between her thighs. "And how do you plan to do that when you're on another floor?"

"Nope, not on another floor," he voice was raw. "I'm between your legs. I'm guessing your pajamas are soft on my skin as I ease your legs open, and come up between them to get at the bottom of your shirt. I move that out of the way so I can kiss your stomach. I love the way your voice hitches when I do that."

Asha's free hand drifted to her stomach, running along the hem of her shirt, fingers lightly brushing the bare skin beneath.

This was so over the line, but she didn't want to stop. Didn't want him to stop.

"Then what?" she breathed.

"I'd keep pushing it up so I could get at more of you. Your ribs, your tits, your neck. I want to taste you, nibble on you, nuzzle you, suck on you. You know, you taste different in different spots. Saltier in that crevice beneath each breast, more like mint along your neck and collarbone where you spray your perfume. Right behind your ear...fuck you're so sweet."

Asha swallowed hard. He remembered all that? Of course, having his voice in her ear as he talked, she could almost smell his cologne and how it had tickled her nose when he'd kissed her throat. She caressed her breast with her free hand, vaguely aware of Dax describing how he would lick and suck at her nipples until they hardened against his tongue. She remembered that all too well—the damp and rough feel of his tongue on her sensitive skin.

"Fuck, Asha. Every time you groan like that, it takes me back to that night, the way you arched your back for me. I could do nothing but kiss your tits all night."

"Dax," she said on a breath. She needed to stop this, stop him, but she couldn't get the words past her throat.

"God, as much as I love your tits, there's something else I've been wanting to do. I'd kiss you just at the navel as I work your bottoms and panties down over your hips. Sliding them down your legs. God, do I love your legs."

"Dax we—"

He didn't listen. Just kept talking. "I want to taste you. I want to lick you until you scream my name. I want to know what you taste like everywhere."

Her core pulsed, even as she eased her hand into her pajama bottoms.

There was a hypnotic quality to the way he spoke, and her

legs fell open as her back arched. The prickly heat of anticipation and longing made her moan. But Dax wasn't physically there to satiate it, only stoke the fire inside her.

She slid her fingers over her slick folds, pretending it was him.

"Are you wet for me, Asha?"

Oh, God, she was so wet. "Y-yes."

"Good. I want you so much. I love thinking about what would have happened if I didn't stop. Would you have let me suck on your clit?"

The velvety, smooth skin was so slick. She stroked herself slowly, sending a shiver of pleasure through her body. She withdrew her hand and shed her bottoms, scooting down on the bed to give herself better access.

She returned to gently teasing her lips and spreading them gently.

"Do you taste good, princess? Do you like it when I tease you with my tongue?"

"Yes, oh, my God."

She wanted Dax. Wanted the weight of him. The long, hard, smoothness of his body. She wanted to know what that felt like for once. *Really* know. She wanted to know what would have happened if he hadn't stopped them.

She slid a finger inside herself, but knew it wouldn't be enough. She needed...more. "Dax, please. I want—" Her body stretched to accommodate a second finger, and she gasped at the sensation.

Sure, she'd touched herself before. A lot, actually, since meeting Dax. But she'd never gone this far.

He groaned, followed by a sharp intake of breath.

"God," she gasped as she tried to reach for that elusive release. Why couldn't she get there? *Because this isn't enough.* "I want your— You feel so... Here. I want you inside me."

"Not as bad...as I want it to...be me inside you. I want...your legs...wrapped around me... Your heels...digging into my ass... holding me in."

Oh God, oh God, oh God, oh... Her release crashed into her, her whole body shuddering as she cried out his name.

On the other end, Dax ground out several curses, his breathing harsh over the phone. "Fuck, fuck, fuck, Asha. *Holy shit.*"

They sat in silence for several minutes, both of them knowing there was no going back from what had just happened. She'd officially broken rule number two... On the phone. Sort of. Whatever. It was bad, because after this there was no way she wouldn't remember his words in her ear.

As her pulse returned to normal and she heard Dax swallowing in an effort to control his breathing, she wished she could roll onto her side and feel the warmth of him envelop her. Like the night he'd held her.

Instead, she felt chilly and thought about the image she presented—legs splayed on the bed, damp with sweat, but ultimately alone. Just like always. For what? She'd followed the rules all her life, trying to be perfect. For once she didn't want to be. She felt a wave of shame threatening to wash over her.

"I miss holding you," Dax admitted. "I liked it."

"Me too," she said quietly in response, closing her legs and curling up with the phone. "But we both know..."

"I know. Still...all you have to do is say so, and I'll head on up there to see you."

The hope in his voice... The temptation tugging at her body... She drew a ragged breath.

When she was finally able to speak again, she whispered, "Goodnight, Dax. I'll see you at breakfast."

"See you then. Sleep well, princess."

SIXTEEN

Dax was perfectly aware that he looked like a nervous teenaged girl waiting for a date to show up. He'd been pacing the lobby for nearly forty-five minutes. To try and look slick whenever he saw one of his teammates, he pretended to be talking on the phone. Yeah, he needed help.

He picked a position where he could see her either get off the elevator or come down the stairs. He had no idea how this was going to go in the harsh light of day, so he figured it might be good to head her off at the pass. *And say what, dumbass?*

Last night was hot, and I want to do it again. No. That was going to make him sound like an asshole. *Newsflash, you are an asshole.*

No. Well, yes, he was, but there was something about her that calmed that burning feeling in his chest. He felt calm when he was with her. And...what the fuck did that even mean?

He wanted to date her? He had no idea how to even do that. He'd never successfully had a relationship. Not to mention all the barriers. Her job. Their team. Her brother. His best friend. His family. It was none of their business, really. But Gramps was a piece of work, and maybe Asha was skittish.

What the hell is wrong with you? You are Dax Coulter. Yeah, but since she'd shown up, he wasn't really getting her out of his head. And he knew this couldn't be a one-time deal. Not that he thought he could get her out of his system with just once. There might not be any getting her out of his system. Not with a girl like Asha. And frankly, he wasn't down with seeing how the other guys watched her.

They thought she was a massive ballbuster. Which was ridiculous. She was smart as fuck. Certainly smarter than he was. That shit didn't intimidate him in the least.

But she wasn't a ballbuster. She just knew what she wanted, and took no prisoners until she got it. He respected that.

It was official. He was a sap. The truth was, he didn't know what he wanted from her. And that was a problem.

Movement caught his eye, and he grinned briefly. He was glad he'd picked his vantage point, because his smart girl thought she could avoid him by taking the stairs. The moment she was out of the stairwell door, he took her by the elbow, and led her down the corridor to the conference rooms he'd staked out.

"Jesus, Dax, you scared me half to death."

Her hair was down today, falling in soft, silken waves down her back. She wore some kind of white wrap dress that clung to her body loosely, but moved with her. And again, heels that made his mouth water. Fuck, the dress wasn't in any way sexy. It was professional. But damned if he didn't want to tug it down to see if her nipples tasted as good as he fucking remembered.

"I'm sorry, but I figured you'd want to have this conversation where no one could see or hear us." He tugged her into a conference room and closed the door behind them.

When he faced her, her pupils dilated and her lips parted slightly. Like she was waiting for a kiss. And fuck, did he want to give her one.

"Dax what are we doing in here?"

He took a deliberate step toward her, and she backed away while licking her lips.

Just one taste. Maybe he'd be able to go a day or two with just a taste. He'd feel better. Less...edgy. "We're talking."

"A-about what?"

"Well, for starters, I want to know if you're okay." Where the fuck had this sensitive side come from? This shit was fucking with his mojo. He was losing his swag. "You know. I needed to see...after what we..." *Shit.* He cleared his throat. "I didn't want you to think that..."

Her cheeks went a deep scarlet, and damned if he didn't want to kiss every inch of her.

"I, uh...fine...perfect... It was..."

"Awesome?"

She exhaled sharply, and her lips twitched with a flash of a smile. "Yes, b—"

Another step toward her. "Good. Because I've been rethinking the other night. I can't get you out of my fucking head, and I think given last night, fighting it is a bad move."

Her eyes went wide. "Dax, you—"

"Hear me out." He insinuated himself between her thighs, forcing the jersey material up higher." I want to taste you. Will you let me taste you, Asha?"

He ran his nose up the column of her throat, and her head rolled back. Why did she smell so damned good?

He placed a kiss at the hollow of her throat, and she shivered. Her little moan made him rock hard. One little sound, and he was ready to go. That was all it took.

But then, she was pushing at his shoulders. "Dax, wait."

Wait, what? He pulled back to look at her properly. Her lips were still parted and soft. Her eyes still dilated and hooded. Her gorgeous breasts rose and fell rapidly as she dragged in a breath. She wanted him. So what was wrong? "Did I do something?"

She shook her head vehemently. "No. God, no." But she still pushed at his shoulders. Fuck. He'd done something. He backed off and gave her space, tucked his hands into the pockets of his jeans. "If I'm crowding you, you just have to tell me. I don't want to pressure you..." He frowned. Had he ever been with someone inexperienced before? He had no idea how to make sure she was okay with all of this.

Asha blinked wide, dark eyes up at him. "No. It's not you. Or rather, it's not what you're doing. Obviously, I...uh...we..." She licked her lips and swallowed hard. "This is chemistry. And uh...yeah. But I think you were right the other day."

"What? No. I'm pretty sure I was a dumbass, torturing us both for no good reason."

She straightened and smoothed out the imaginary wrinkles in her dress. "Dax, I like you. I mean more than just..." She pointed a finger back and forth, gesturing between them. "I *know* I'm not your type."

He frowned. "What the hell is that supposed to mean?"

"Sorry. I'm awkward. I don't know how to do this."

He forced himself to drag in a deep breath. "It's fine. Say what you need to say."

"Like we talked about. This is...uh...intense. And I think it's confined quarters, and I'm not really the kind of girl you're used to, so, I'm a challenge, and it's probably better if we can stay on good terms. You know, friends."

He was a walking, talking, jumble of hormones, and she wanted to be his...*friend*.

"You're saying you don't feel this?"

"Oh, I feel it. I just think you were right from the start. We can't do this. This is a chemical thing. And it'll pass." She cleared her throat. "I feel things with you. And it makes me reckless, and it terrifies me. You'll get bored and move on."

The hell he would. "And that thing last night? In the elevator, on the phone?"

She flushed again. "I think, maybe...we maybe limit our physical interactions? And I'm way out of control with you. I mean, I've never done anything like..."

He could feel his lips tip into a brief smirk as she spoke. She felt the same thing he did. Except her solution was to run, and his was to face it like a game of chicken with oncoming traffic. It was okay. He could wait. Because by now, he got it. She was working her way under his skin. "So what, you want to pretend it didn't happen? That hasn't worked for us, exactly."

Asha ducked her head, that dark hair of hers acting like a veil. "No. I'm just trying to manage this the best way I know how. I like you. And once we get over our, initial...differences... Let's just say, I can see why Damon thinks of you like family. You just don't want anyone else seeing that." Dax shifted on his feet. She saw too damn much. "I'd like to keep working with you. I'd like to be friends. But, if I can feel it when you watch me, I know someone is going to notice. So, for both of our sakes, we need to chill."

He nodded slowly. They could do it her way, for now. She'd come around eventually. Because he knew something that she didn't. They were under each other's skin. And it wouldn't be going away. No matter how much she wanted it to.

THE NEXT WEEK, DAX KEPT TO HIS HOTEL ROOM IN THE days leading up to the game in New York. Practice, massage, room. Only talking to Asha on the phone. And even then, she was back to business. Like she hadn't given him the hottest orgasm of his life without even being in the room. For the millionth time, he pushed that particular memory away, knowing it would be back before he knew it, and thought about football, instead.

The Thrashers won again that Sunday, and by far more than just a field goal.

Dax's numbers were better than the week before as well, but he took a hard hit in the last minutes of the game, and the team's trainers insisted he be thoroughly checked out before heading back to the hotel.

Asha was waiting for him when he finally emerged from the locker room.

"They said I'm good to go," he told her, calming the concern on her face. "Going to have a headache for a while, but they cleared me for concussion."

She frowned as she worried her lip. "Are you queasy at all, or do you think you could go for something to eat?" she asked, still eyeing him warily.

"Pizza," Dax said with certainty. "I want pizza. We can pick it up on the way back to the hotel, and then we don't have to worry about going out."

"Sounds...nice," she said, her voice tinged with sadness. "We should each get one to take back to *our* rooms," she said, making a point of clarifying.

Damn. Okay. Fine. He had time. There was no rushing this.

They were in the parking garage, and Asha's rental car was in sight.

"You don't trust being alone together?" He kept his voice low.

"Do you?" she asked, the flush in her cheeks somewhat concealed by the shadows around them.

"I guess not," Dax agreed.

They called from the car and picked up their orders en

route, making sure to be seen by some of Dax's teammates, getting off the elevator on their own floors with their individual orders. Dax noticed a few significant looks exchanged, but most of the guys restricted themselves to asking about how Dax's head was feeling.

"Left my ears ringing, but that touchdown at the end there was worth it," he said, grinning at them as he struggled to open his hotel room door with one hand.

He slid the pizza box onto the dresser next to the television, and stripped off some of his extra layers until he was comfortable. Why was it impossible to get hotel rooms to the right temperature?

After he grabbed a slice of pizza and the remote, he sat on the bed to watch highlights from the day's other games. His cell phone rang, and he glanced over to where he'd left it, plugged in on the bedside table. It was Asha.

"What can I do for you?" he asked, his mouth full of melted cheese.

"I was watching the highlights and was wondering if that play you guys ran in the third quarter, when you were third and six from the twenty-seven-yard line, was the same as the one you outlined for me a few weeks ago?" she asked, her words coming out rapid-fire.

Dax swallowed as he struggled to shift gears mentally. So she wasn't calling him to beg him to come to her room. *Damn.* "Which play?"

"They're going over it on channel...forty-nine. I had to mute the guys on the TV, 'cause they were distracting, but their diagram looks like the one you drew."

Dax flipped the station to see what she was talking about. Sure enough, there was the route they'd run in the third, where he'd managed to score a touchdown.

"Huh, they really are breaking it down."

"You sound surprised," she said. "They seem to think it was a pretty good play. 'Sophisticated', I think what's-his-name said a minute ago. How close is it to the one you showed me?"

"Well..." he trailed off, watching the muted commentators debate the play. "It's...pretty close."

"But you guys changed some things in it, didn't you? That's what they're talking about now."

"Yeah. Just a few tweaks." Ellis had been unhappy to hear something new.

The news network had their computer simulators running through the original play in yellow on the screen, and then they adjusted the play to what the Thrashers had run that afternoon in green, to highlight the differences.

"So, whose tweaks were they?" Asha asked, breaking Dax's concentration.

"What?"

"I asked who tweaked it?"

"Don't remember," he muttered, his neck getting hot from all the scrutiny.

"Liar," Asha laughed.

"You're calling me a liar, princess?"

"Yeah. 'Cause you're lying. This play has your fingerprints all over it. That little fake there in the middle? That was something you mentioned when I was asking you my questions. It's a great play, and it's yours. Own it," she told him.

Dax was glad she couldn't see him blushing over her praise. "It is kind of awesome to see them picking it apart like this."

"You need to keep it up. You've got a gift for it. Use it. If you don't want to come out with it right away, that's fine. But if you enjoy it?" She paused and he could picture her shrugging in his mind's eye. "You never know where things are gonna go. Look at those guys on the screen. They all had careers on the field, but for one reason or another, they had to give up playing. But they still found a way to work in an industry they love."

"Are you saying you think I should be on TV?"

"I'm saying you *could* be. Or you could be a coach someday. Or work in an organization at the administrative level," Asha listed off.

"Is this because of the hit I took today?" he teased, uncomfortable with the serious talk about his future beyond football. "I told you I'm fine and I plan on playing for a while."

"I know you will. But if you have a plan, you'll be ready for your brother's wedding, and all the questions you'll get from your family," Asha continued before he could interrupt. "It's one of those things that's bound to come up at that kind of family function, and it's exactly the kind of question that makes you go all...Dax the asshole. Anyway, you can use something like this to impress the fam and get them off your back, leaving you free to actually *enjoy* the day."

"My brother's wedding? Is *that* what this is about?" he asked. Her mind worked too fast for him. Especially when he had a headache.

"No," she said. "It's just one of the directions my mind headed in while watching them talking about the play."

"Can I ask what the other directions were? Please say my lips between your thighs, please say—"

Asha laughed. "Well, if you want to know every stop along the way... I could tell you it was your play, and that had me thinking about how to market your newfound talent. Whether the team would benefit from pushing you to the foreground that way, or if it would be more effective to keep it under wraps for a while. It fits with the marketing strategy for you, individually. Your grandfather wasn't particularly known for his strategy on the field, more in the boardroom after starting Legacy Sports. Of course, thinking about your family and marketing got me going on the issue of the bye week in a few weeks, and how it coincides with Bryce's wedding."

"That sounds exhausting. How can you think of so many things at once?" He laughed and crossed to the coffee table where he'd left the pizza, to grab another slice.

"It's a blessing and a curse. Anyway, back to the subject of Bryce's wedding," she continued, redirecting the conversation. "Do you know who'll be covering it? Big bosses are looking for a few different plans on how to handle it. Obviously it's the bye week, which means you won't miss play time, but it also means there won't be as much team news and they don't want to be getting fed stories or watching the standings. They want to be *making* stories."

"And my family is the story they have in mind?" He couldn't keep the defensive tone from his voice. "So much for not trading on the Coulter name," he muttered.

"Come on, Dax," she laughed. "Give me more credit than that. I already told them the angle they wanted wouldn't fly. Most of them are married, and they know better than to try and take focus away from the bride and groom on their wedding day. But apparently, they needed to be reminded by a *woman* before they agreed not to do it."

He heard her scoff and he relaxed. "So what do you have in mind?"

"Make it about your brother and Tami," she said. "Emphasize that you're there to be his best man and that it's their day. It's already going to be covered by the sports media. And probably the larger media as well, given the Legacy Sports connections. So let them deal with it. Leave you in your role as your brother's best man and emphasize *that*. That this is a *family* thing and when you're with them, *that's* who you are. A brother, a son, not just the football machine they turned you into. Your whole family gets marketed for athleticism and the business side of things but you guys are still a *family,* and your professional achievements aren't your entire lives."

Dax snorted. "Good luck telling that to Gramps," he muttered.

"Okay, sure, not everyone can turn it off, but that doesn't mean we can't turn it off in how we present you," she admitted. "Anyway, I wanted to have a direct contact to whatever media people might be there so I can worm my way in with them to... guide them...and maybe get dibs on some of their candid shots from the wedding. From what I gathered of Tami when I met her, she's going to be sure there's a tight leash on anyone there who might be inclined to publish random details and pics. So I didn't want to go stepping on toes to try and get anything specific. Shots of you with your brothers, or during your best-man speech, or whatever."

Suddenly, he remembered. *The speech.*

"Shit! What am I supposed to do for that speech?"

"I can listen to whatever you come up with, if that helps," she offered.

"Actually, that would be good." he agreed. "But I've got to come up with something first. Maybe if I ask Echo... She'll have an idea of where I can start..."

"Got any funny stories about Bryce from when you were little?"

"What?"

"You know, pranks he played on you, pranks you played on him, that sort of thing."

"Maybe. You think funny is the way to go?"

"I think funny is always a good way to start," Asha explained. "It's also how everyone will expect you to start. And then you segue into something more sentimental and deep, and you've got everyone eating from the palm of your hand."

He sighed. "Funny I can probably manage. Sentimental..."

"You can be very sweet if you put your mind to it. Just, sometimes, you come off as…"

"What? I come off a little what?"

"Distant. Or flippant. The sentiment is there, but you could use a little…finesse." The hesitation was still in her voice. "I don't mean to be too blunt, or mean, or anything. I can be the same way a lot of the time—especially when it comes to talking about…you know…personal stuff. Feelings and all. But if you wanted to bounce your ideas off me, I can help you find that right balance, you know?"

"Actually, I think I do." There was a pause during which he could hear her chewing on her pizza while he chewed and swallowed a few more bites of his. Dax pondered his next step, before taking the plunge.

"So, how about instead of getting you Tami's information so you can ask her about the wedding thing you wanted, pictures or whatever, how about you be my date and get them yourself?"

Silence…then chewing and swallowing on Asha's end. *Probably buying herself time*, he thought as he suddenly became very aware of the way his heart was pounding in his chest. *I shouldn't have said that—shouldn't even have thought it. She's off-limits. I promised I wouldn't say or do anything—*

"I'll have to clear it," she finally said, breaking the silence and exhaling, long and hard. "But if I frame it the right way, they'll probably okay it. They'll be more comfortable with *someone* there to keep an eye on things and give a full report, and I am the one assigned to you."

"If you're not comfortable—" he said, backtracking instinctively.

"Well… I mean…it's not that I'm not *comfortable* or that I don't want to go. Your family were all really nice—er, random insensitive comments notwithstanding. But if *you* don't think it's a good idea…"

"I asked you, remember?"

She sighed. "And I want to be there with you...but I'm not sure we *should*."

Dax stayed quiet, waiting. She was probably right. They shouldn't do something like that when they didn't even trust themselves to have pizza alone together. *But* they wouldn't be alone. There would be a country club full of family and friends who would be watching everyone and everything. Surely they could trust themselves when there were witnesses around... Built in chaperones, as it were.

Asha might have been thinking along the same lines, because she finally broke the silence. "I'll talk to them tomorrow. It's still three weeks away. If we change our minds...I can fake the flu."

Dax grinned. "I'll let Bryce know."

SEVENTEEN

Getting approval for attending the Coulter-Ivey wedding from her bosses was easy. Asha simply suggested one of them should go. Take on babysitting and get what she needed. They'd immediately offered her up as sacrifice.

During the next two weeks, she and Dax continued to carry on their professional relationship predominantly via phone. Yes, okay, so totally a chickenshit thing to do, but given that she could feel him simply when he walked into a room, it was probably for the best. They talked about everything from work, to team gossip, to what they each thought of the newest pizza place to pop up in town. The fact that her parents planned to come for a visit. In all that time, if she didn't call, he would. Sometimes with a family anecdote, or just to hear her voice. More than once she fell asleep to the mellow timbre of his words.

They only met in person on game days, when it was necessary to do so, and they managed to make sure that other people were present, so they could make a point of publicly demonstrating their professionalism.

The locker room rumors about what might or might not be going on between them were still circulating, but the teasing air about them had dissipated. And as far as Asha knew, the rumors hadn't gone beyond the players themselves. Everyone had other things on their minds. Winning was having a positive effect on all their spirits. Back from their road trip, they'd played two home games—both of which were solid wins against division opponents, increasing the Thrashers' chances of making it to the post-season. The fact that anyone was even talking about them in conjunction with the post-season had sent an excited buzz through the organization. Attendance was up during both of those games. The second markedly higher than the first.

For their next road game they were only headed to Miami, so even though it was technically away and they had to travel, the shadows weren't required to follow and keep an eye on them.

The freedom and aura of an improving season sent many of the players out to the clubs, even though their curfew was still in place. Instead of going out, however, Dax called Asha.

"You're forgoing a night out?" she asked, adding an incredulous tone to her voice. "Are they making snowballs in hell?"

"Shut it. I'm too busy talking to you, and trying to comprehend why you would ever ruin Nutella with bananas."

She giggled. "It's delicious."

She paused, thinking. It was probably a bad idea to bring it up, but something had been bugging her since she'd gotten off the elevator with some of the team earlier that morning.

They'd been all talking about where they were headed that night. Ignoring her, like they usually did, they happily chatted about where to go to pick up women, and which one of them was going to get laid. She should have been more affronted, but the truth was, she was used to it. Most people ignored her, or deliberately left her out of conversations. This time she was glad to be left out. Until Ellis mentioned Dax.

His name alone was like a forbidden flame, and like a moron, she flew directly into it. *Every. Damn. Time.*

And one of the comments had stuck with her all damn day. She'd overheard Samuels say, "Don't bother asking Coulter. It's like the dude doesn't even smash anymore."

Dax's voice was soft. "What? What is it? You seem like you want to ask me something, but you're afraid to. I can tell."

Asha sighed. "I'm just thinking about something Samuels said."

"Oh yeah?"

Now or never. Stop being a coward. She cleared her throat. "He said, uh, that you don't smash anymore."

Dax coughed. "What?"

"Smash. I assume it means you're not sleeping with anyone. Or maybe that you don't party."

"He said this? In front of you?"

"I was in the elevator with them. I'm invisible to those guys, remember?"

"I—" He hesitated. "He means I don't hook up anymore."

Her heart slammed against her ribs. Hold up, now. "Why not?"

He swallowed before putting the lid back on the tub of Rocky Road. "What you said at the beginning of all this mattered to me. I want to change the image of what people see. Besides, I haven't been all that interested."

"Again, why?" She had no idea what the hell she was doing, or why she was even asking. There was no way this conversation could go anywhere safe.

"You ever do something because it's a habit? It's just what you've always done, so you keep doing it and doing it, and somehow, you wonder if you ever liked doing it in the first place?"

"Oh, I've seen the great Dax Coulter in action. You like the party."

His words tripped out slowly. "I do... Though for a while now, it's felt like a habit instead of something I really *wanted* to do. The women, the drinking. I think we can both agree it's not been working in my favor. I figured I'd try my hand at something new. And I realize, I kind of like it."

"Good. I like this version of you." Wisely, she refrained from adding more. The problem was, she liked this version of Dax a lot. As in, she was starting to fall for him. He was funny. Sensitive and sweet. She liked being his friend. Liked being around him. And she had a feeling that developing a soft spot for him was going to get her hurt.

"Nervous about the wedding?" she asked, changing the subject.

"Well...yeah, just a bit. I don't mind being in front of people, but I'm not a huge fan of *talking* in front of them," he confessed.

"You do fine in the post-game interviews," she assured him.

"That's football talk. I can talk football 'til I'm blue in the face and never get tired of it or run out of things to say. This... this is serious, and it's a big deal. Bryce actually trusts me. I'm not screwing this up."

"You won't screw up." She leaned back against the cushions of her sofa. "You'll be fine. Just look for me when the time comes, and I can mouth the words to help you along if you need it. Like a cue card or something."

"More like a bad high school play," he said, laughing.

"It won't really matter that much in the long run—everyone will be paying attention to Bryce and Tami, and as long as you don't put your foot in your mouth, which is impossible with that speech, by the way, you'll be fine. Just don't worry about sounding like a robot, or reciting it off notecards, because it's clear you put a lot of thought into it, and everyone will be able to see that and will appreciate it." She reached for her soda and took a sip. "As long as you make either the bride or groom cry good tears, you'll be a success."

He laughed again lightly and paused before adding, "Thank you." He paused again. "I know it's...uh...we didn't... Things." She could hear him swallow. "Thank you."

"You're welcome," she whispered, feeling a twinge somewhere in the center of her chest. She was *too* close to him. It would hurt when he finally got bored. But she couldn't let go. Not yet.

EIGHTEEN

Shit. This was so fucked. Dax was sweating like he'd been doing 3 a days in the Jacksonville summer heat. He'd never been so nervous. And *he* wasn't the one getting married.

Bryce laughed at him as they stood at the altar. "Aren't you supposed to be the one calming *me* down?"

"What do you have to worry about?" Dax asked with a smile. "You and Tami are great together, and you're going to be fine. *I'm* the one everyone's expecting will somehow manage to fuck things up."

Bryce shook his head. "Do you have the rings?"

Dax checked his pocket and pulled them out, along with the notecards for his speech, giving both a final glance before putting them back. "Yes."

"You'll be fine. Just...find something calming to focus on, and pay attention to that. I'll nudge you when it's your turn for something," Bryce promised.

Dax nodded, looking out into the growing sea of faces, and his hands shook. His parents and grandparents were seated in the first row, their heads bent in conversation. His mother was tightly holding his father's hand and she already had tissues out, crying quietly as she watched the two of them. His father looked tired and old in a way that struck Dax hard.

His parents were getting older, but it was easy to overlook that, next to the vigor demonstrated by his grandparents. But even they weren't as foreboding as he once found them to be.

As he watched them, Gramps' gaze focused on him, meeting his eye. Dax was familiar with most of his grandfather's facial expressions, but there was something different about the way he was being examined this time. It wasn't the usual disappointment or disgust. He wasn't sure what it was that was different. Maybe that was it. There was uncertainty in the old man's eyes. Something he'd been convinced of, sure about, had been altered and he was trying to decide what to do about it.

Whatever his conclusion might be, the attention was making Dax uncomfortable.

He shifted his attention back to his father, but caught sight of Asha sitting on the other side of the church. She'd opted to sit on Tami's side, having befriended her rather quickly on the only other occasion they'd met, and in an effort to balance out the seating in the church. Tami had no close family, and most of her friends were friends she had in common with Bryce.

Asha wasn't wearing anything like what he'd seen her in before. She wore purple this time. Her dress still hugged her curves, but it had some panels that flowed out over her legs making it look like she was floating. She'd pulled her hair away from her face but it still hung loose, secured by something that sparkled the same way her dress did. She was looking over her shoulder to the entrance where guests were pouring in at a suddenly steadier rate and filling up the rows of seats. She shifted and turned her head, camera in hand, snapping photos of the flower arrangements spaced evenly along the outer ends of the rows.

Dax relaxed as he watched her. After a few moments, she

turned and caught him staring at her. She smiled, made a face, and then raised her camera to snap a shot of him with Bryce. His brother laughed below his breath.

"What?" Dax asked, finally looking away from Asha.

"Nothing." Bryce watched him with a sideways look until Fox and Gage came up, having handed over ushering duties.

"What do you mean nothing?"

His brother laughed. "I'm just wondering if you know how you feel about her yet?"

Dax rubbed at the burning spot in his chest. "She's great. Awesome."

Bryce just kept laughing.

"What is it?" Dax asked with a frown.

"Just that I want to be a fly on the wall when you do realize it. You're expression is going to be hilarious."

"Tami and the bridesmaids are here," Fox whispered as he straightened his boutonniere.

All four brothers tensed as a hush fell over the church and people made it to their final places, ready to begin.

Dax's eyes found their way to Asha again. Her attention, along with everyone else's, was on the bride waiting in the wings for her cue. Everyone's attention except Dax's. Bryce was right. He loved that girl. Which meant he was so totally screwed.

ASHA WATCHED AS DAX MADE HIS BEST-MAN SPEECH, mouthing the words along with him, happy that while his gaze frequently found its way to her, he didn't seem to be lip-reading, but rather seeking her out for reassurance.

"To my big brother, Bryce, and my new sister, Tami," he said in conclusion, raising his glass of champagne. "When you know, you know."

There was a round of applause and the sound of glasses clinking, while Bryce and Tami rose so they could take turns awkwardly hugging Dax from across one another. Asha and a slew of other guests snapped photos.

Then it was Amy, the maid of honor's turn to speak, and Asha set her camera down and took a few more bites of her piece of the wedding cake. The dinner, speeches, and formalities were nearly over, and soon the plates would be whisked away so the dancing could start.

She was only half paying attention to Amy's speech. Something about Tami using a tennis racket to beat up a mugger. Instead, she glanced around the room, amazed at just how different it looked from when she'd crashed the high school reunion with the Coulter siblings only a few weeks earlier. The lighting and table decorations played a huge role in the change, but there were fewer tables as well. It was a much more intimate affair than she'd imagined it would be.

She found herself watching the table with Dax's family gathered around. His parents and grandparents each held on to each other. His mother rested her head against his father's shoulder. His grandmother had an arm around his grandfather. There was something mutually possessive about it, each staking a claim to their partner as they watched Bryce and Tami, sitting close with their fingers intertwined, always finding a way to maintain physical contact with one another.

I want that. And she did. Hell, a boyfriend would be great. A real one. What she was doing with Dax, it didn't count. And it was stopping her from doing what she came to do in Jacksonville. Open up. Broaden her horizons. She spent all her time with him, and he wasn't an option. Besides, he might want her, but he didn't do relationships.

Asha rubbed a hand up her bare arm and fiddled with the sheer over-layer of her dress with its glittery beading, picking at a loose thread in the stitching while she swallowed and took a few deep breaths. She knew part of the problem was that she was sitting by herself.

Well, not truly alone, but with a handful of other guests who were strangers to her, at a table of mismatched leftovers. The guests who they couldn't be sure would come, along with the plus ones, whose dates were a part of the bridal party or were otherwise occupied. Of course, she wasn't really a true guest for the wedding. She wasn't Dax's formal date. Deep down she knew *that* was part of the problem. She wasn't really lonely, in the sense that she was desperately single. And she was frustrated, because when she was with Dax she wasn't lonely at all.

She'd been lying to herself. She *wanted* to be with him.

Clapping and further toasting shattered her introspective moment. She gulped the champagne in her glass, the bubbles tickling her sinuses, and further scattering the broken thoughts of a few moments earlier.

Bryce and Tami headed for the dance floor to share their first dance.

She was so busy watching the happy couple, she missed Dax as he snuck around the head table to sit in the empty seat beside her. She clapped a hand over her mouth to stifle the yelp she let out when she saw him.

"Sorry," he whispered.

"For making me jump out of my skin?"

"Well, that, and for kind of abandoning you here like this. When I invited you to be my date, I wasn't thinking about the seating arrangements or anything like that."

"It's fine," she assured him. "It's kind of a work thing, so it's not a big deal. Not *any* kind of deal. At all."

He glanced down at his hands, nodding slowly but saying nothing and Asha's face heated. She was glad he wasn't looking at her in that moment, because they were getting dangerously close to—

"I don't care if it's a work thing for you or not," he said, interrupting her train of thought. "It's also a wedding, and as a guest, you should be having a good time. So," he said, rising with a quick look to the dance floor. "Dance with me?"

She turned to the crowded floor then back to Dax. His eyes wandered over her, searching. He wanted her and she wanted him.

She stood and took his hand.

NINETEEN

The sparkly things on Asha's dress pressed into Dax's palm as his hand found its place at the small of her back, drawing her body closer to his. At first, she was stiff in his arms, forcing them both to maintain the rigid distance dictated by their professional relationship, but the slow music and dim lighting lulled them closer together until there was no space left between them. Asha rested her cheek against Dax's chest, and he heard her breathing him in. They were embracing and swaying more than they were dancing, but they weren't alone in that position on the dance floor.

Dax gently rested his chin against Asha's temple, content even though the contact had started a low simmering in his blood.

"What's wrong?" Asha asked, her hold on him tightening.

He smiled down at her and shook his head. "Nothing," he whispered in her ear. She tucked herself back into him. He was so scared. He was totally in love with her. How the fuck had that happened?

The sudden knowledge made him dizzy.

His hold on her tightened, and she squeezed him back. It

wasn't that anything was suddenly possible, or that the weight was being taken from his shoulders. Rather, that he'd found a different way of breathing through it all, and the desire to please other people had taken a backseat to the need of being able to live with himself. There was a new font of strength he'd tapped into, and it made the weight less noticeable. She'd done that.

He was happy with that. He was enough.

Dax could sense someone watching them, and he looked up to lock eyes with his grandfather. Rather than shrink under the older man's gaze as he'd been doing from habit for years, Dax refused to look away. The unfamiliar thing in his grandfather's eyes was still there, and he still didn't know what it was. Or maybe it was the champagne talking. Maybe Gramps had simply let himself get caught up in the festive air of the wedding and was actually letting himself enjoy things for a change.

The song ended and Asha pulled away, the warmth that had been between them cooling, and leaving Dax with the feeling that something was missing. He clung to her hand and leaned down to whisper in her ear. "Interested in taking a walk? It's a bit warm in here."

"Sure. Let me get my shawl."

While he waited for Asha, he sidled up to Echo.

"What's up, sis?" he asked, startling her. He watched her face shift into what he thought of as "show mode". A strained smile and tired crinkling near her eyes. She looked tired, and not just because of the stress of the day—there was something else causing her cracks to show.

"Nothing," she said, dismissively. "Just...the usual, you know. Bryce is married now. Makes me wonder which of us they'll be pushing to settle down next," she teased half-heartedly. "Probably you, since you're...well...*you*."

He scoffed. "Me? I'm a notorious player with a reputation to uphold," he countered, his words sounding hollow even to his own ears. "I'm the troublemaker who can't be trusted not to screw up my own life—I certainly can't be trusted not to screw up someone else's, too."

Echo laughed. "Please. You're coming into your own now, and everyone can see it."

"You don't have to worry about coming into your own," Dax told her. "You've been here for a while, haven't you?"

Her next laugh was more of a cough. "Yup—that's the job of the only daughter, isn't it? Take care of things because the boys can't be trusted to think of anyone but themselves? It's about time you all caught up to me." She drained the rest of her champagne.

Dax noticed her gaze kept finding its way back to their parents.

"Is everything all right with Dad?" he asked, watching her tense up before cocking her head to one side.

"He's just tired, is all. The company's been keeping him busy. When Bryce got hurt and it wasn't clear he'd be able to play again, Dad talked himself into bringing Bryce on. Bryce, of course, had different plans, and Dad's still got all that company stuff on his plate. Having to deal with all the wedding stuff hasn't helped," Echo rambled. "He'll be fine, though. It's under control."

"I didn't realize he had to do so much for the wedding," Dax said, studying his sister. Her stance indicated there was something off about what she said. He couldn't believe she was outright lying to him, so maybe she wasn't as reassured or certain about what might be going on as *she* wanted to believe.

"Bryce and Tami took care of a lot of the details, but they couldn't be here in person for much of it, obviously. Dad and Mom and I stepped up and stood in for them a bit where they needed us to." She shrugged. "Now, is there something else you're interested in picking my brain about, or are you just trying to avoid your date?"

"She's..." He started to say she wasn't his date, but that wasn't entirely true—nor did he want it to be true. "I'm not sure what she is," he finally admitted.

"She's good for you," Echo told him, matter-of-factly. "Like Tami's good for Bryce." She nodded to where the newlyweds were wrapped around each other, foreheads pressed together as they danced in a tight circle, oblivious to everyone else around them.

"She is," Dax agreed. "But I'm afraid it's a bit more complicated than that."

Echo shrugged. "You'll figure it out."

"What makes you so sure?"

"You wanted to follow in Gramps' footsteps and take on football," she pointed out. "None of the rest of us had the courage to try that."

"What about you with the running? He did that, too."

"He didn't love it the way he loved football. I know it's been hard on you—*he's* been hard on you. But look at you now. Like I said—you'll figure it out."

Asha appeared with her wrap draped around her shoulders. "There you are. Lost sight of you along the wall for a bit, there. Hi, Echo."

"Asha." Echo grinned at her. "What do you think so far?"

"It's lovely. So beautiful. Still, it's getting a bit warm in here, so we were going to head out for a walk and some fresh air. Wanna come...?"

Echo flashed a grin to Dax, who shot daggers back before she laughed. "That's okay. I haven't been out dancing as much as the two of you."

"We'll see you around again, I'm sure," Dax said as he moved to Asha's side. He ushered her through the door, into the chill air of early evening.

Finding their way outside was easy, but with the sun having set so early, it was impossible to find their way around the grounds.

"Didn't you grow up near here or something?" Asha teased. "Shouldn't you be familiar with all the ins and outs of the club?" Her affectation was enough to have them both laughing.

"Yeah, well, this place wasn't exactly our playground," he explained. "Now the grounds at the big house... Those I still know like the back of my hand. I could be blindfolded and find my way around there with only minimal destruction. I snuck in and out so many times..."

"But there would still be *some* destruction..."

"Well, sure. I'm taller and broader than I was then," he said, puffing out his chest as she laughed. "My gauge for the distances is bound to be a bit off."

"There's light that way," Asha pointed. "Why don't we go investigate? It could be a garden, maybe..."

They hurried along the brick path to find themselves in an illuminated area.

"Or the parking lot," she grumbled.

"If we can find the car, we can at least get in and get warm."

"The whole point of this little walk was to cool off," she reminded him, her teeth beginning to chatter audibly. She pulled her wrap tighter around her shoulders just as they found the car where the valet had parked it.

Shit, now or never. He just prayed he didn't crash and burn.

"I'm tired of trying to play it cool when it comes to you," he blurted out.

She slowed beside him, and he turned to make sure she was still there. He'd been waiting to get this out. Waiting to tell her. He braced himself.

She stepped forward and rose on her toes to kiss him.

"Me too," she breathed against his lips when she broke away to catch her breath.

He wrapped his arms around her, drawing her warmth against him and enfolding her in his. She melted into him for a moment before finally pulling back.

"So you said something about a car and getting warm?" She took his hand and led him past the rows of parked vehicles. She stopped in front of the rental she'd driven to and from the church earlier that day, pausing at the door to fish the keys from her clutch.

Dax moved in so that she was backed against the side of the car. "It's not that cold out," he insisted, pressing himself against her, sharing his warmth with her. She turned to face him, wincing as her backside met the cold metal of the car.

"You had other ideas for warming me up?" She said with a sly smile.

He dropped his forehead to hers. "Jeez, I want you. But not in the backseat of a car. My timing sucks."

"No. Your timing is perfect."

The moment Asha's lips pressed against his, Dax took over the kiss. She wanted him too. And she tasted so damn good. Angling his head, he kissed her deeper, as he tucked her flush against him, needing her closer.

Dax braced her against the car and cupped her face, his senses going into complete and total overload. She was everything perfect he'd been waiting for.

And he didn't want to screw this up. He pulled back and searched her gaze. "You are so beautiful. Do you even have any idea?"

She ducked her head, and even in the moonlight, he could see her soft flush. "You make me feel that way."

"Well, it's easy because it's true." He kissed her again and she slipped her hands inside his jacket and around his waist. Just a light touch from her was enough to elicit a shiver. He was not going to make it if a simple touch was enough to have him begging. The wind blew strands of her hair into their faces with the slight chill.

Asha pulled back. "I have heard that body heat is the best way to stay warm in cold weather."

Dax couldn't breathe. Body heat. Oh, man. He would kill to have her hands on him.

But they were in a parking lot. Yes, they were hidden by the tall shrubs. But still. "We should go. You know get inside somewhere."

Asha shook her head. "You know, I've never made out in a car before."

Made out in—? He couldn't help the smile tugging at his lips. "Is that so?"

She nodded with a wide-eyed innocence that made him want to laugh. "I always wondered what it would be like. The possibility of getting caught. Even *I* have to admit, it's a little sexy."

Dick, meet steel. Yeah, she was going to kill him. She rocked her hips into him and popped the top button. "Asha, anyone could come out." Was that his voice? Why did he sound so strangled? Probably because all his blood was rushing to his dick right now.

"I know. I just want you to—"

Fuck it, he was tired of trying to be so well behaved. When he kissed her again, he was less controlled. More desperate. Pouring every ounce of need into the kiss.

His tongue slid over hers as he licked into her mouth. And he demanded that she respond to him, demanded that she meet his need with her own. He wasn't disappointed.

She clutched the front of his shirt and tugged him close.

When she popped another button to slide her fingertips over the exposed flesh, he was more than ready to show her every dirty fantasy he'd ever had about her.

With every sexy mewling sound she made, she popped another button, until his shirt hung open. Asha dragged her lips from his to look at him, and Dax tried desperately to catch his breath. Tried to find some kind of even ground, following the emotional free-fall of kissing her.

Asha stared at him for a long moment before tracing her fingertips over his abs. When she licked her lips he would have sworn he could come just from watching that.

"Dax?"

"Mmm?" He'd find real words later. *Much later*.

"I want you to touch me."

"My pleasure." Dax pressed her into the door of the car as he kissed her again. His hand bracketed her ribs, his thumbs tracing over the fabric of her dress. When he reached the underside of her breasts, he could feel her holding her breath. Every sense went on red alert, his body so attuned to hers. Balancing precariously on the same frequency, waiting for that hum of pleasure and need to sync.

When he traced his thumbs over her nipples her back bowed and she cried out his name. "Dax... Oh, God."

"Yeah? Baby?" Fuck, he would give anything to always hear his name like that from her lips.

"More, I want more."

Shit. Swallowing hard, he traced circles on the stiff peaks as he angled to kiss along the column of her throat. She smelled so damn good. With her dress, it didn't take much for the fabric to give just enough to release her nipple. When his thumb came into contact with her soft flesh, he groaned. The tingling in his spine started to spread through his body, making him hum with need and lust, making it too hard to think. All he could see was this woman. All he could see was her and how she made him feel.

He plucked the soft tip between his thumb and forefinger, and her nails dug into his chest and shoulder. "Dax, oh God."

He bent his head to take the exposed tip into his mouth, and her hips jerked to meet his. *Yeah, baby, your body knows what to do. You know what you want.* He picked her up to position her better. Her dress bunched higher on her thighs as he made room for his bigger body. And then he ducked his head and sucked the raspberry-colored tip into his mouth. Damn, so sweet. So damn... His cock nestled into the juncture of her thighs, and he lost his damn mind. With a tight grip on her hips, he helped her find a rhythm as she ground onto his cock.

Yes. Right there. Her heat rolled over the length of him. Even with the several layers of clothes between them, he could feel the searing fire of her core. Driving him mad with the tease, making him want everything from her.

With a frustrated growl, he tugged the other side of her dress down and molded his hand to her full breast. Testing the weight, kneading her flesh. He was a leg man any day, but Asha's curves. *Damn.* She was converting him. He'd been dreaming for months of touching them. Sucking on them... fucking them. Fuck, the mental picture of his cock sliding back and forth between her tits had him shaking.

When he released the one with a soft *pop*, she whimpered. "Easy baby, I'm an equal opportunity guy. I just want to kiss this one, too." As he took her other soft peak into his mouth to suckle, Asha dug her hands into his hair and held him tight.

"Dax. I just...I-I want..."

"Yes, tell me what you want. I'll give it to you," he whispered against her breast.

"You. I want you. Inside me. I have to know. I've—it's been—I can't... I don't want to wait."

"Asha." He groaned. "The first time we make love is not going to be in the parking lot at my brother's wedding. At the very least, we're going to be in a bed."

"Dax..."

"That's my condition, baby."

"But I feel like I'm burning up."

He nodded. "I know. Together we're..." He couldn't even find the right words. There weren't any.

"I just need to feel...something," she whimpered.

Ah, she needed more friction. Well, he could help her with that. "Mmm, you want me to touch you."

All he could feel was the nod against his chest as she writhed in his arms.

"Like the first night I kissed you. You liked that."

"Y-yes."

Dax swallowed hard. He could give her this. The problem was, if he touched her, he'd want to taste her, too. All over...to discover all the secret places on her body and make her scream his name. And he sure as hell didn't want to use just his fingers to touch her. He wanted to use his tongue, his dick. "Fuck. I want you so bad I might actually explode."

"I want to touch you too, Dax."

Hell. As if he needed that kind of encouragement. The thought of Asha's hand wrapped around his dick in the elevator. It made his damn legs shake. Dax hitched up her dress inch by inch, exposing more thigh. Her skin felt like the softest satin. He had to be gentle. He didn't want to leave marks on any of that perfect, pretty skin.

When he reached the edge of her thong, he cursed low. The fabric was soaked. She was so wet. Already so ready. When he slipped his thumb under the elastic and over the baby-smooth skin, his eyes damn near crossed.

"Jesus, Asha, did you wax? Was this for me?"

He could feel her ragged breaths against his chest. "I assumed we'd be swimming as the weather was so nice, but then...I sort of hoped...maybe you'd want to kiss me again."

"Keep hope alive. I know I have." He gently traced his thumb over her clit and she bucked arching her back into the car.

"Dax? What are you doing to me?"

"Me? You're the one who's been peeling away every layer of me, and laying a piece of yourself over my soul. I can't go to bed without dreaming of this. I can't wake up without wishing for this. A stolen second or two where I might be good enough for you." Their words gave way to gasps and hushed, muffled whispers, as he traced slow, lazy circles. He wanted her so wild she begged. He wanted all of this to be good for her. He should fix her dress, take her inside, say goodbye, and then take her to her hotel. Somewhere private. Where he could take his time. But he was powerless to stop touching her. Powerless to stop what was happening with them.

"You've always been good enough. I just didn't know I could dare want this."

As if there was a universe in existence where he would not want her. "All you have to do is tell me what you want. If I can give it to you, I will."

She lifted her head and gazed up at him from under dark lashes. "I want to feel you."

He frowned. "You are feeling me." To prove his point, he circled her clit again and she hummed. "See?"

"No. I mean *you*. No clothes between us. I want to feel you moving against me. That night. In the hotel. And now it feels so good. I'm curious."

"Jesus, Asha." He dropped his forehead to hers. "We need a bed. And condoms. I don't have any on me. Obviously, I didn't think this was ever happening. And I'm not taking you against the car. I'm just...not."

"And I don't want you to. I just want to...play. To feel you, that's all."

"And I will be coming inside of a second against these pretty soft lips. I'm not taking risks with you. We need condoms."

"Dax, I've been on the pill since I went to college."

"Asha—"

"Please, Dax." She reached for his buckle. The clink of the metal on metal rang loud, so loud in the silence of the night. He held his breath when she undid the metal claps of his tuxedo pants and reached inside his boxers. *Yes, God. Fucking yes.* His cock jerked in her hands, ready and more than willing to do whatever the fuck she wanted. And screw what Dax had to say about it. *Traitor.*

Her gaze didn't leave his as she freed him and guided him to where she needed him most.

As soon as the head of his cock met the soft satin of her panties, he jerked. Pre-come oozed from his tip and Dax shook as he fought the orgasm. *"Fuck,"* he grunted through gritted teeth.

"I just want to feel. Please."

Her voice in that soft, pleading tone was his undoing. Before his brain could assert what was right and wrong, his thumb hooked in her panties and dragged them aside, exposing her sweet center to the rigid length of him. Positioning himself just so, he slid along her petal-soft lips from root to tip.

He growled, she hissed. But they clung to each other, locked in a world of their own making, where they played their private game and didn't give a fuck who might wander by a darkened corner of the parking lot.

This was risky and dangerous. And just the sort of thing the old him would do. This was not Asha for damn sure, but the bliss of her softness was enough to make him not give a shit.

The slow slide of his cock over her folds, then the drag of the tip over her clit. *Slide. Drag. Slide...drag.*

Her head snapped up, and the next thing he knew her hips picked up the rotations, bringing her over him again and again. Her last motion had her lifting up just a hair, and gave brand-new-fucking-meaning to *just the tip*.

And then she was coming. All wide, dark eyes, and teeth dragging over perfect, full lips. And nails digging into his shoulders... And she looked fucking amazing.

It was when she focused her dark gaze on him and reached between them to stroke him that he lost all control of the reins, no matter how much he'd pretended to have them. As he came in her hand and over her satin smooth lips, he knew. Asha Wix, the innocent, had ruined him.

TWENTY

It didn't occur to Asha to suggest they go back to her hotel until they were coasting up the long driveway to the large Coulter estate.

"Oh, I thought we'd be going back to the hotel."

Even though she'd only been inside once before, it struck her as strangely quiet. Of course, the rest of the family was still at the wedding, but there had been others moving about the house—a cook and a housemaid or two, if she remembered correctly. But then, they probably had the day off—or at least would have gone home for the night by now.

Dax left most of the lights off, as he led her up a set of stairs and down a hallway before ducking into a room and throwing the lights on with flair.

"I didn't get to give you much of a tour last time, but this...is my old bedroom."

"Funny how the tour starts here," she laughed.

The space was smaller than she'd imagined. The thought was clear enough on her face for him to read it there.

"Mom and Dad wanted us each to have our own rooms. So they opted for smaller, individual rooms rather than larger ones that had to be shared," he explained. "There're two bathrooms, one at each end of the hall."

He reached behind her to close and lock the door, grinning at her. Asha giggled and dropped her wrap to the floor, before kicking off her heels. Dax had off his shoes, socks and jacket before she got her hands on him. He walked her backward to his bed, kissing her deep and tugging on the zipper of her dress.

"Asha, I promise, next time, I'm going to take my time. Fucking hours, but right now, I need to be inside you. Quick."

Her slick core contracted. She wrapped her arms around him, angling up to his neck. He groaned into her mouth, his erection hard and throbbing between them.

She smiled against his lips, then squealed as he picked her up easily and tossed her in the center of the bed. Following, he took the fabric of her dress up, exposing flesh as he went. "I am going to burst, Asha. You have been driving me nuts since I picked you up."

Even as he tugged off the rest of her dress, she begged him. "Dax, hurry."

"I am. I'm just distracted by how pretty you are. So damn soft. I want to taste you. Can I?"

Oh. Wow. She nodded even as she arched her back, and he rewarded her with a lick directly on her clit. *Holy shit.* Moist heat flooded her center before she could even enjoy the ride.

But he wasn't done. With his big hands, he parted her thighs and growled low as he lapped at her. Lick, stroke, tease. Fuck her with his tongue. Tease her clit. Dax Coulter knew how to seduce.

Asha tried to hold on for the ride. But the orgasm chased through every nerve ending, and threatened to engulf her. But then suddenly, when she stood on the precipice of bliss, he pulled back.

"Dax, oh my God. So...close."

His expression was harsh, ruined, brows down, eyes hooded, but vulnerable, bare, raw. "I know, but I want you coming again around my cock."

They both tore at his clothes. She went for his shirt, he went for his buckle. But he got distracted, rubbing his hands up and down her thighs, fingers digging into her flesh as he sought to bring her closer. When her hand wrapped around the length of him, his eyes crossed and he squeezed them shut. "Fuck, that's so...good."

"Are you sure? I don't really—"

He wrapped his hand around her wrist. "Too good. I want to come all over your hands again. All over your tits, your ass, your pussy. I want to mark you again and again and again. But first, I want to make love to you, so you need to stop."

Asha stilled her hand, but fascinated, rubbed her thumb over the head of his dick, like she'd done that first night as she teased and kissed him. She lingered, sucking on his lower lip.

"You're such a cock tease, deliberately making me crazy."

"I don't have any idea what I'm doing. I'm just doing what I've been curious about. I wanted to know if this would make you snap."

Dax narrowed his eyes. He couldn't wait any longer. Dax reached into his bedside drawer and thanked God he still had condoms in there.

As she continued to rub pre-come on the crown of his dick, he tore open the foil. Gently, he eased her hand off and she frowned. She'd wanted to...help. Making quick work of the condom, he lay between her legs, searching her gaze. "I do anything you don't like, you tell me immediately."

"Dax. Just please— I need—"

She was trusting him with this. Trusting him to take care of her. She loved him. Had loved him. And she wanted this to be his.

As he rocked into her, Dax watched in amazement. Her eyes went wide as her silken, hot sheath tightened around him. But then she smiled.

Dax pushed himself up on to his elbows so he could see her face. He wanted to watch her. Every expression. Every breath. When she wrapped her legs around his back, his cock slid deep, and he had to break the eye contact as he fought for control.

Her nails dug into his shoulders and his back, and she made little gasping sounds in the back of her throat. But it was the one word that broke him. "More."

Fuck. He picked up the pace, the sweet glide of coming home followed with the ache of retreat.

Shit. Yes. So tight. So good. So... Oh, fuck he was going to come, and she hadn't come again. With a none-too-gentle tug, he yanked down her strapless bra, and dipped his head to suckle her dusky nipple. When she arched her back and slid her hands into his hair, tugging gently, he teased the sensitive flesh with his teeth.

He registered the quiver first, then the way her nails scored his scalp. And then, of course, there was the low chant of his name. "Oh God, Dax. Please...Dax... Yes...there. Oh, God." And then she clamped around his cock like a vise, and she was flying.

"Fuck, Asha." As he watched her and his release shuddered up his spine, he knew the truth. This was where he belonged.

He held on to her tight, burying his face in her neck.

"I'm never letting you go." Oh, fuck him. Had he just said that? He would run her off before they even got far.

Her breath hitched and he waited, the burn of rejection starting in his feet, then working its way up.

Asha pressed her forehead to his. Then in a quiet whisper said, "Good. I won't go."

He lifted his head and searched her gaze. He saw it there.

The vulnerability, the trust. And something else he couldn't identify.

He kissed her then, long and deep, his arms tightening their hold and closing what little space there was between her bare breasts and his chest. She slid her arms around his neck, and snaked her fingers into his hair.

She was his. Why did that knowledge simultaneously make him feel like a giant and also terrify him?

She used her grasp on his hair to pull his head gently back and away from her. "You know this complicates things," she said.

"I don't know," Dax said, as he slipped out of her and eased them down onto their sides, their bodies still a tangle of limbs. "It seems to me like it's the only thing that makes sense. We'll work it out. Right now, I'm going to enjoy holding you."

She smiled, nuzzling her head against his shoulder briefly, before falling asleep.

He watched her for a while, praying he didn't fuck this up.

Asha woke sometime in the middle of the night, with Dax's fingers sliding in and out of her slick core. Her back against his chest, his hard cock pressing into her ass, she gave a sigh, arched into the covers, and parted her thighs. He lifted her leg and slid along her, until he was in position to enter her once more. She winced at the initial sting, but the pain soon gave way to pleasure, as he stroked her clit. This lovemaking session was different. Slower, more tender. Like low embers giving way to an inferno.

"We really need to—" she started, then angled her body for easier, and deeper, penetration. She wound her fists into the sheets and pillows as his large hands cupped her breasts, thumbs teasing her nipples.

He froze as her words sank in, and she reached back quickly to reassure him. "Don't stop. That's not what I meant. Please, God, don't stop what you were doing," she panted.

He chuckled. "We need a condom. I only meant to tease."

She froze. Condom. Yes. Holy hell. They absolutely needed one. She was on the pill to help regulate her cycle, but still. He rolled away, and before she knew it, was sliding back home again. His fingers trailed down the side of her body, tickling her ribs, on their way to the warmth between her legs right near where they were joined. "I get tested every six months, Asha but I would never risk anything with you. I slipped just now. And back at the car. I really wasn't thinking. You feel so damn good." His fingers searched for the spot that would undo her in his arms.

She nipped at his bottom lip. "We both got carried away."

Dax pressed a kiss to the side of her throat, as he pressed a finger to her clit and made her whimper.

"I thought we needed to go to back to my hotel. You know, before we get caught."

"You let me worry about that." He gently pinched her nipple and she moaned. When she canted her hips back, he slid in, hard and deep.

For once in her life, she was just going to let go. "Okay, you're in charge."

His breath tickled her ear. "I love the sound of that." His hands tightened in her hair. As he made love to her, he continued.

"I don't want to have to worry about where...and when I'm seen with you...what we're doing together," he told her, his fingers digging in deeper as he quickened his pace and brought her rapidly to the edge, pushing her over so that she cried out. "I love you, and I'm not going to stop touching you."

Asha held her breath as the words sank in. He loved her? "Dax, I—"

He shook his head. "Shhh. Let me show you how much. He kept up the pace, his erection rubbing against her G spot again and again.

"Dax," she whispered.

"Yes, princess?"

"Don't hurt me."

He paused only momentarily. "I would sooner cut out my heart. I'm not letting you go." He circled her clit again, triggering another wave of pleasure.

After falling asleep again, Asha woke with a start, and glanced at the bedside table. No alarm clock. She scrambled into a shirt she found on the bedside table. The lower hem reached her knees, and the sleeves hung down to her elbows.

"Mmm...what time is it?"

"It's almost three a.m.," she replied. "Shouldn't your parents be back from the wedding by now?" she asked, switching to a whisper. "Your brothers and sister?"

"They're probably in bed," he said with a shrug.

"Right, we should go." she said. Now, where was her underwear?

"Still waiting for the blood to get back to your brain?" Dax asked with a chuckle. "I know mine's resistant to making the journey north."

Asha laughed before moving back to the bed and folding her legs carefully beneath her. Right. Now to fix this, so they'd both make it through.

"I have to go to HR," she said. "It will be better to talk to them before the rumors get going again. To come clean on my own is my best chance of keeping my job. If I don't act like I've got something to hide, then they'll know I can be trusted. Besides, my work speaks for itself. I know I'm not the only one who's contributed to the turnaround. You guys all seem to be gelling well with the new coaches—but the way the major networks' commentators have jumped all over your plays—"

"Well, before any of that, I need to tell your brother," he muttered.

"It's none of his damn business." She didn't need her family having an explosion about this yet.

Dax cocked his head and rolled his eyes at her. "Will you get over that, already? That's *not* the reason I want to be the one to tell him about us."

Asha crossed her arms over her chest. She wished, once more, that she was wearing her underwear during the exchange.

"He's my best friend," Dax continued. "If he had a new girl he was crazy about, I'd like to think I'd be one of the first people he'd tell about it."

Asha's mouth twitched with the impulse to smile, but she resisted.

"*I* think Damon *might* tell his family first," she challenged.

Dax laughed at that, shattering more of her resolve. "And I'm sure he told you guys about Cindy? Brooke? What about Tabitha?"

Who the hell were those women? Asha pursed her lips.

"Look, *I'd* feel better if I'm the one to tell him. I know that who you sleep with is up to you, and I'm *thrilled* that it's me. But to Damon you're still his little sister, and he's *not* going to want to hear about your sex life, least of all if it comes with a lecture from you. And also, he's not going to be happy it's me. I'll take the brunt of his yelling."

Dax's hand found its way to Asha's bare leg, massaging it gently, inching higher and higher. She reached out and laid her hand over his, stopping his progress to twine her fingers with his.

"Focus," she scolded, and smacked his wandering hand.

"He's not going to think *anyone* is good enough for you. Especially me," Dax continued, a more somber note in his voice. "He knows me. My track record sucks. No one knows me better than Damon. Except maybe you," he amended. "But you know me *now*. Damon knows how I *was*. Everything I did in college, everything I'm...ashamed of...he doesn't just know about it, he was there. Telling him...it'll help to *show* him how much you mean to me."

Asha's anger dissipated. He needed to do this. She might not like it, but she understood that need. "If his approval means that much to *you,* tell him. But if you let him push you about breaking up with me because he *doesn't* want us dating—"

His brows snapped down. "I'm not giving you up without a fight. I finally get someone to want me as I am. No way I'm walking away."

"I don't want a fight," she reminded him.

"Then I'll tell him to talk to you, if he has a major problem."

"Damn right."

His brow furrowed. "But...I think we need to hold off on HR. It'll be better after the season. Then it's not on their time card, and they can't bitch too much."

"Dax, I think—"

He put up a hand. "Hear me out. You've worked so hard. The regular season is almost over. After that, we have time together."

She knew what he wasn't saying—what if this didn't work, and she'd risked everything? "But if they find out..."

"We'll be careful. On away games, video chat. At home, we'll make it work. Just give us time."

"Well...I don't *want* to lose my job over our relationship. I don't *think* I will," she said slowly and carefully. "But if it came down to one or the other..." She shrugged. "There are other jobs and I have amazing letters of recommendation in my portfolio that all explain how talented I am," she assured him with a smile and a kiss on the cheek. She felt him smile beneath her lips before he turned his head to kiss her properly.

"Besides," she added, breaking away. "I spent some time chatting your folks up at the wedding. Your father seemed intrigued by some of the ideas I had for Legacy Sports. If I do get fired, I'd be willing to bet I could talk him into giving me a job with the company." She was only half kidding, but the expression on Dax's face told her he didn't like it.

"Just for a little while, until after I deal with Damon, at least. Please."

She didn't like it, but she could hold off. "Okay, but we're going to keep discussing this."

He nodded. "Of course. But first..." He shut her up with another kiss, this time laying her out on the bed while his hands slid up her haunches to her bare ass, and suddenly, she was extremely glad she wasn't wearing panties.

TWENTY-ONE

Having a plan in place wasn't quite the same as enacting it. In the harsh light of day, the prospect of doing so had him hesitating. Damon was going to end him. But it was so fucking worth it. She was perfect.

"I don't care if your family knows about us," Asha reassured Dax. "But I'd rather not let it get out publicly."

"Have your stuff sent to the airport, then," Dax suggested, pulling on casual clothes and watching Asha's cheeks redden as she searched the floor for her underthings. He lifted the jacket of his tux from the floor and found her crumpled panties, holding them out for her until she snatched them away and turned her back to wriggle into them. "You went to a wedding and the party ended later than you expected—or the party moved, and you went with it. There are plenty of ways to explain it, so stop worrying."

He grasped her by her upper arms, holding her in place long enough to plant a kiss on her forehead.

"Relax. It'll be fine."

"And when exactly are you planning on calling Damon to let him know?" she countered.

Dax felt his stomach drop, but fought to keep his features controlled. "It's...not something I want to...over the phone," he muttered the words with difficulty. "I'd rather tell him in person. No chance of him hanging up on me, then," he said with a half-hearted laugh. *Much greater chance he'll punch me in the face, though*, he added to himself.

"You're going to wait another four weeks to tell him, *after* you guys play the Pats?" Asha's voice was skeptical and accusatory. "If I go to HR tomorrow and they give me the okay on all this, would you be willing to keep things...innocuous between us until you tell him?" she asked, slipping her arms around his waist, pressing her body against his and rising to her toes to kiss him softly, sensuously. Her fingers gripped him tightly as she slid against him in a carefully calculated manner— he could feel the rough sequins and beading of the dress' sheer top layer through the worn fabric of the T-shirt he'd thrown on —the one he'd given her to wear in bed during the night. He struggled to keep his thoughts on her question, but found his mind wandering to whether it was clusters of beads he felt or her hardened nipples—he couldn't remember whether she'd put her bra back on before slipping back into her dress. She must have—why wouldn't she?—but he slid his hands up her back, feeling for the clasp under the fabric just to be sure.

She laughed and pulled away. "I didn't think so. But we'll have to keep being discreet until you tell Damon, since you're so insistent it be you."

He watched her amusement drain as she looked at the locked bedroom door. If his family had started moving about in their morning routines he hadn't noticed, but he was immune to their noises after so many years. Honestly, he was more put off by the silence of his apartment in Jacksonville than anything. He always had something on that provided background noise.

"I know I want this," she said quietly, and he was only half sure she was talking to him and not herself. "I know I do. I just... I want to skip the next part. I've seen it happen with Sam. I've seen it happen with Damon. It's the worst part of any relationship, don't you think? At first it's just the two of you, and there's that bubble. Then you have to *tell* people and deal with all the 'I told you so's and the 'what're you thinking's and everyone judges your relationship, tells you whether it's a good thing or a bad thing, the right thing or the wrong thing. But after everyone knows...you don't quite get back to the bubble, but the comments and the looks...they go away. After a while everyone just...accepts it, and it can just *be* again."

"Okay. How about this? Just check with HR about what the policies are. Don't reveal anything. You'll be more comfortable. I just want you happy."

"Are you sure?"

Dax nodded. "Yes." Her nervous gaze was still focused on the door. "We're doing this." He walked over to it and turned the lock, then the handle, before pulling it open.

"Pop," he said, shooting her a smile.

She looked from the empty hallway to him, her expression brightening when her eyes came into focus.

"Pop," she repeated, taking a deep breath and stepping out of his room.

"Ms. Wix?" Mrs. Cusack's voice was confused, as she looked up to find Asha standing nervously before her desk. "Did we have an appointment?" The older woman began rifling through papers on her desk, searching for the datebook she used to keep track of everything. No matter how many times she entered meetings on the computer's calendars, no matter how many reminders and alerts she programmed, the only thing that she trusted completely was writing her appointments down.

"I don't have an appointment, no," Asha confessed. "I just hoped you would have a few minutes, and we could talk." Mrs. Cusack visibly relaxed.

"Well, then, what can I help you with?"

"I mostly just wanted to have a little chat, you know..." Asha had thought of so many ways to start the conversation, and she had decided the best thing to do was to just quickly say what needed to be said. Rip off the bandage, as it were. Looking down into Mrs. Cusack's inquisitive and cheerful face, Asha was too afraid of being judged by the woman.

"A chat?" Mrs. Cusack asked, leaning back in her chair the way Asha imagined a therapist might. "What would you like to chat about?"

"I just...I feel like with the switchover—all the people let go, all the new people hired, people like me—there was a lot of information being thrown around, a lot of policies and rules and 'this is how things are done,' and I was given so much stuff to read through and sign..." She could feel herself rambling and gripped her leg tightly through her skirt—dug her fingernails into the soft flesh and tried desperately not to think of the marks Dax's teeth had left there—to make herself stop. "I had some hypothetical situations that I was looking to get your opinion on —things that...might come up, or that... I just want to know what my options ar—would be. Information is power, right?" But she couldn't make herself laugh at the joke.

She couldn't decide whether Mrs. Cusack looked worried or amused by her obvious discomfort.

"You can go ahead and shut the door if you want," Mrs. Cusack advised, pushing herself up and out of her chair. "Would you care for a cup of coffee? There's muffins back here, too," she told Asha, as she waved a hand to invite her deeper into the odd configuration of offices that comprised the Human Resources department.

"Um...sure. I'll have a cup."

"Blueberry, banana nut, and chocolate chip." Mrs. Cusack waved to a plastic container where the muffins were housed, before handing Asha a cup of reinforced cardboard and directing her to the coffee pot. "I'm afraid we don't have decaf in these parts."

"Full strength is fine. So uh...about these hypotheticals..."

"Have you been, hypothetically, experiencing sexual harassment in your workplace?" Mrs. Cusack asked tactfully.

She blinked. "What? No. I mean, well, *yes,* but not more than I can handle or than I expected. And anyway that isn't what I wanted to—" Asha stammered, caught off guard by Mrs. Cusack's directness.

"Before I hear any of your hypotheticals," she interrupted Asha, holding up a hand, "let me take down your complaints so that we have them on record."

"But I didn't come to make any complaints," Asha objected.

Mrs. Cusack reached out a hand and gripped Asha's forearm gently, giving her a squeeze to emphasize her point. "I find it's often a good idea to make a record. Whether you mean to file a formal complaint or not. Just so they are already *on the record* if there is ever an issue down the road." She spoke slowly and with her eyes locked on Asha's. "It's a recommendation I make to *all* employees who come with questions."

But especially the female ones. The words hung in the air, unspoken. Or at least, that's where Asha's mind went as far as finishing the sentence.

"Right... yes... instances of—got it," she nodded and watched Mrs. Cusack relax in the conviction her meaning was clear.

"Here," Mrs. Cusack said with a smile and a wave of her hand. "Have a seat and we'll get started."

"So what is this? I thought we were doing hypotheticals." Dax asked a few days later when they were able to spend some time together at Asha's apartment. He was leaning on the bar top between her minuscule kitchen and what passed for a dining area, the pages she'd received from Mrs. Cusack spread out before him.

"You have to read through it and sign it," Asha explained as she pulled glasses and plates from the cabinets. "Turns out, so long as we sign paperwork releasing the team, the administration, your coaches, my bosses, basically signing our souls away and vowing not to sue should things go south, they don't care what we do to each other in the bedroom." She grinned and waggled her eyebrows suggestively. "Matter of fact, given your *extensive* porn collection, I might be interested in spanking."

He wasn't paying attention, his brow furrowed as he read through one of the last sections again. "What's this bit here?" He held it out to her, pointing at the section in question.

"Oh, I had them put that part in. It means that we get to publicize our 'theoretical' relationship when and how we like. Basically, they can't out us to get attention for themselves, and when we *do* make our relationship public knowledge, all they can officially do is issue a statement saying they're aware of it," she explained. "*We* get to be in charge of us. No one else." She leaned across the counter to kiss him. "But I didn't give them a name. I just said if this were to ever happen, they needed that clause. I was vague. But they aren't stupid."

"Everyone's asses are collectively covered?" he asked, peeking over the counter to double-check.

"For now, anyway," she teased. "That can wait until after we've had dinner. I went to the trouble of cooking, and I'm not letting it get cold."

TWENTY-TWO

Their relationship blossomed in relative privacy during the next few weeks as the Thrashers continued to win with greater reliability, crawling their way up the standings until they were battling it out in the wild card race.

The week before Christmas, they were set to play Damon and the Patriots, who were securely in the playoffs with their spot at the top of their division. The game garnered a lot of attention in the media, as announcers proclaimed it the Thrashers' true test. With Dax's steady performance on the field a must-mention subject whenever they discussed the Thrashers' remarkable improvement, the fact that he would be playing against his former teammate did not go unnoticed.

"Do you think it will be a happy reunion, or are you worried that he's going to have your number?" a reporter called out during one of the post-practice press conferences.

Dax declined to sarcastically point out the fact that he and Damon were both offensive players, so they wouldn't *actually* be playing on the field at the same time, despite the strong impulse. Whenever he was stressed, it was harder to suppress his old instincts.

But it wasn't the upcoming game that was stressing him out. And the image Asha had worked so tirelessly to help him build meant too much to throw away with a flippant response now.

"Damon and I go way back. We're great friends. And he's a consumate player on a world-class team. We're going to have to work really hard to get ourselves ready for them, and we'll just have to see how things go on Sunday and see if we can't stash a few surprises up our sleeves," Dax said with a grin, hoping he exuded more confidence than he felt.

He was dreading the coming weekend, but had already called Damon to see if he'd want to get together for dinner or drinks after the game and Damon had enthusiastically accepted.

That night in bed, Asha said, "I wish you wouldn't worry so much." Despite the fact that it was an away game, Asha had volunteered to travel with the team, though curfews for the players were more self-imposed now than reinforced. Superstition and a significant winning streak trumped personal preference when it came to the players' traveling habits.

The buzz around the game necessitated someone from the PR department be on site, and with Damon on the opposing team, Asha had been the logical choice. Especially when confronted with the reality of her colleagues' eagerness to spend time with their families and attend to holiday-related obligations.

Dax reached across her to grab his phone from the stand by the bed. He had been careful to wait until after the hotel's exercise room had closed for the night and his teammates had all turned in for the evening before sneaking out of his own room to meet Asha at hers. He wanted to be sure he snuck back before anyone was likely to be up and about in the morning to avoid jumpstarting the rumor mill—he would be able to stop hiding the truth from them soon enough—he just had to tell Damon, first.

"It would have been over by now, if you'd just sucked it up and called him weeks ago," Asha reminded him, nuzzling playfully into his neck.

Dax sighed. "I know. I'm wondering now if maybe you weren't right about that," he admitted.

She laughed. "Oh, I know I'm right. I always am."

"Oh, really? What about when you said we couldn't be together? That it would ruin your career?"

"I *believe* I said we *shouldn't* be together because it *could* ruin my career," she emphasized. "And it still might, so don't go jumping all over that point just yet. It's just that...well, I do love what I do, and my career means a lot to me, but having you makes it even better."

"Whether that's what you said or not doesn't change how right you are here, either way," Dax admitted, shaking his head but dropping the point. "I know I shouldn't feel guilty about..." He inclined his head toward her lying naked beneath the sheets. His gaze locked on her nipple and he licked his lips. Maybe if he just licked it that would be enough. Who was he kidding? They'd be finishing this conversation with him inside her.

"Sleeping with your best friend's sister," she finished for him.

"And I don't, not for that, at least. I know how I feel about you, and I know it's..."

"Undeniable? Irresistible? Mind-blowing?" she offered as her hand traced its way down his chest to slip beneath the covers pulled up to his waist. He pressed a hand on top of the blankets, catching hers as it passed over his navel. Her immobilized wrist didn't stop her fingers from playing with the trail of hair that led from his navel farther south. Dick. Hard. Just the tease was enough.

"Let's stick with the first one. My intentions are...honorable," he said. But they certainly weren't *pure*. "But it's been a few weeks now, and...I feel like he'll be upset because I didn't tell him. That that will be worse than whatever he might blame me for, as far as *this* is concerned." He slid his hand up her forearm, under the blanket, turning and bending toward her so that the tips of her fingers came into contact with the smoother parts of him—there was still plenty of time before he had to slip back to his own room. He had to learn some control with her.

"If I were Damon, that's what I'd be upset about," Asha said, bringing her hand back up to rest against Dax's chest. Her tone wasn't one of triumph any longer, but rather one of sympathy. "But he'll get over it. He's still your best friend and he wants you to be happy. He wants me to be happy, too. Once he sees it, he'll get over it. I'm sure he's seen you do worse."

"True...but nothing that felt like a personal betrayal."

Asha kissed his throat and slipped her hands up the back of his neck into his hair.

Dax groaned. "Is this you trying to take my mind off of this, or are you just hoping I'll shut up?" The bliss mixed with desperation.

She giggled, grinding against him sensuously. "Bit of both. Is it working?" she asked, knowing full well that it was. "How about if I tell you I don't want to use condoms anymore?"

Oh, fuck. His cock slid along her slick entrance and he cursed.

"Asha—"

"Please, Dax. I want to feel you. Now."

Teeth clenched, he slid home with nothing between them. Oh, shit... He was going to— She groaned low, and her velvet walls clenched around him, milking him to bliss.

"What's the matter with you, Coulter?" Coach Mills hollered at him after he reached the sideline and grabbed his water bottle. "Get your head in the game or I'll take your ass out to join it on the sidelines."

"Yes, Coach," he grunted as respectfully as he could. Samuels gave him a sympathetic pat on the shoulder, while most of the rest of his teammates on the offensive line turned their attention back to the field, where the special teams unit was in position to punt the ball.

The game was tied, and they were in the fourth quarter where every second, every play counted. *And* he'd literally dropped the ball. If he'd been able to keep hold of it as he hit the ground, they would have at least been in field goal range, if not in possession of a first down, and another chance to get farther down the field for a touchdown.

They needed their defense to stop the Patriots. If not altogether, then at least hold them to a field goal, with enough time left to have another scoring play of their own.

Dax closed his eyes and did what he could to block out the noises of the game and the fans around him. He held his helmet in his hands, the plastic of the outer shell cold in the December air, but solid between his fingers. He kept telling himself it was the cold that was affecting his hold on the ball, and not his preoccupation with Damon and what he had to take care of *after* the game.

He set his helmet between his feet and rubbed his hands together, blowing warm air into the hollow between them and feeling the pins-and-needles response of his nerves coming back to life.

There was a loud commotion on the field and the fans in the stands were voicing their displeasure over something. Dax looked up to see a large pile of players, with officials blowing their whistles as they fought to discern who had control of the ball at the bottom.

The Thrashers had it. They'd recovered a fumble, and now they were down to three minutes on the clock with a tie game.

"Get back out there, boys," Coach Mills ordered, as Dax bent to retrieve his helmet.

He headed onto the field and listened to their quarterback Seth call the play. A running play, so he'd be working to draw some of the defenders to the side, in hopes of clearing a lane for their runner.

It worked enough to get them another first down, and then they hit the two-minute warning.

They were stopped on the line of scrimmage the next two downs, but got another first down on the third, running down the clock and bringing them into field goal range.

Their quarterback was sacked, and they lost four yards in the process. They were also down to just thirty-five seconds.

"One more play to get better position for the field goal, and whatever we do, we need to get that clock stopped. Run out of bounds as soon as you catch it," Vic said, looking first to Dax and then to Samuels, who was supposed to block for him, but had caught a ball or two when Vic's passes fell short of their mark.

The ball was hiked and Dax took off, dodging the defender who was covering him with a double fake to the left, then right. Once he was past him, Dax looked back over his shoulder to find the ball right where it was supposed to be.

He grabbed it out of the air and turned forward, his eyes on the white paint of the sideline a few steps away. But the field in front of him was open, except for one defender coming toward him from the side a few yards up the field. In a split second, Dax turned away from running toward the sideline and instead, shifted his feet to run right at the defender barreling toward him. The defender was larger, heavier than Dax, which meant he would have a more difficult time changing direction; his momentum wasn't going to change.

Dax was just a few feet from being in the defender's grasp—his arms were opened and ready to close on Dax as soon as he was in range, or at least make an attempt to bat the ball away.

Dax pulled up short and jumped, bringing his legs up as high as he could, knees to his chest. The defender missed, laying himself out and falling to the ground, while Dax landed on the other side of him, and ran all out toward the end zone.

It was a twenty-yard pass with an eighteen yard run from the point he caught it to score the touchdown. The clock had just two seconds left by the time the Thrashers went to kick the ball back to the Patriots, and the game was over.

Amidst all the excited and congratulatory pats on the back and punches to the shoulder were at least as many 'what the hell were you thinking' and 'you're lucky that worked' comments.

Coach Mills looked at him with narrowed eyes, and Dax knew he'd be making up for his improvisation by running extra laps in practice. He nodded to the Coach, who nodded in return. The acknowledgment was enough to allow both to continue celebrating in the moment. The teams mixed a bit as the players headed for the locker rooms. Dax was just inside the tunnel when Damon found him.

"You're a lucky bastard, you know that," Damon said as he smacked Dax between his shoulder blades.

"Lucky in so many ways," Dax agreed with a grin. "You guys played well. You always do. It's what makes beating you feel so good."

Damon rolled his eyes.

They'd reached the spot in the hallway where they were supposed to split up and each head to their own locker room, but they hesitated. The area was growing increasingly deserted as everyone pushed to get through the post-game necessities so they could head home or to their hotels for dinner or bed or whatever else they planned to do that night.

"Listen, man," Dax began, taking the plunge. "There was something I wanted to talk to you about. I was going to wait 'til we went out to dinner but... I know that you said you wanted me to keep an eye on Asha for you, when she first moved to Jacksonville and started working for the team, and I have. That is, I've tried, I mean, *I* think I have, but I also know it's probably not the way you meant..." He babbled for a while before he noticed Damon was laughing.

"Keep going," Damon encouraged. "This is pretty entertaining."

The tension rolled out of Dax's shoulders when he realized Damon already knew.

"She told you, didn't she?"

Damon shook his head. "Not really. Well, not explicitly. She's my little sister," he shrugged. "I know how she gets. And it was all about what she *wasn't* saying. Besides, I have her on the Find My Friends app. She spends an awful lot of time at your place...at all hours of the night. *And* she *did* tell us about how she had to travel with the team and shadow players for something they were working on and that you were one of the guys she had to shadow. Well, once I started to see how *you* were acting, it was clear something was up with you and I figured you'd tell me what it was if you felt you could and if you couldn't..." Damon laughed as Dax struggled to figure out whether what he was feeling was disappointment, elation, or just simple relief.

"You're not mad?"

"I mean, I don't want to think about it. Because—ew—but I know who you are. You're a good dude. Even if you don't see it."

"I have to admit, laughing *was* on the list of reactions I thought you might have when I told you. Of course, in every scenario I pictured where you laughed, it was right before punching me." Dax was dazed, but the adrenaline from the game and his anxiety began to dissipate from his system, leaving him feeling heavy and tired.

"I can do that if it'll make you feel better, but I think it'd be best to wait 'til we're not still technically at work," Damon offered.

"You're really not mad? Not upset I kept it from you for so long?"

"Well, how long *have* you been seeing her?"

"Officially or unofficially?"

Damon's posture grew a little tense. "What do you mean by *un*officially?"

Dax swallowed. "We...wanted to see each other for a while..." he said slowly. "But we didn't think it would be...appropriate. Then we...we just had no fucks to give. *That's* when 'officially' started, but there were lots of calls that we pretended were work stuff that were just an excuse to talk and... Well, you *did* want me to keep an eye on her for you, so there were a few dinners, but those were all above board..."

Damon blinked slowly, much of his earlier amusement fading away. "You know...I don't need the details on this one."

"I wanted to be the one to tell you," Dax continued. "I made Asha promise she'd let me do it. But I didn't want to do it over the phone, and with our schedules..."

"You told me," Damon said with a nod. "That's what matters...*and* it shows just how much you care about her. Which is even more important."

"I love her," Dax confessed.

"Well, you know you're already like a brother to me," Damon reminded him. "And, as Asha has been reminding me for a while now, it's not my place to tell her what she can or can't do, who she can or can't see, and even if she appreciates my opinion and approval, she doesn't need them. Besides, you know that if you hurt her, I will end your life."

"Yup, I know. *I* will end me," Dax said. "Of course, you had us all figured out."

"What really surprises me is that you've managed to keep it out of the press for—no, I *really* don't want to know *how* long or just where you've been, or what you've been up to that's kept you two off everyone's radar," Damon shook his head, preferring ignorance.

Dax obligingly held his tongue and pressed his lips into a straight line. No deets was a good call. Now that Damon officially knew, they just had to tell his family. Now that would be fun. They probably wouldn't believe it.

"So give her a call and have her join us for dinner," Damon told Dax, breaking into his reverie with a tilt of the head. "You know she's waiting by the phone to find out how this all went." He turned to head toward the Patriots' locker room, while Dax turned toward the visitors' side. "Oh, and Dax?" He paused and waited for Dax to glance back over his shoulder. "Remember what I said. I know all kinds of ways to end your life." He winked and grinned.

Dax nodded, pretty sure Damon was only kidding...maybe.

TWENTY-THREE

"Thanks for walking me to my room, Aaron. It's not necessary, I promise you." While those were the words that exited Asha's mouth, what she meant was, *Time to go dude, you've been lingering and hanging on for far too long.* There'd been a quick, impromptu meeting of the marketing team to talk about the playoffs, and what to say to the press, as well as the rapid-fire opportunities for community face time that had come up. Management wanted to strike while the iron was literally still in the fire. Aaron offered to walk her back to her hotel room, and there'd been no gentle way no let him down without saying "I'm dating a player" so...here she was.

He leaned against her door. She couldn't tell if he did it to be obnoxious, or if he just didn't realize that all she wanted to do was get in her room and get the hell away from him. To be fair, it wasn't him exactly, she just wanted to call Dax to see how it went with Damon. To see if they were still on. Or find that bra and panty set he liked so much and get dressed for dinner. Yeah, pretty much all thoughts centered on Dax right now, and she certainly didn't have the patience for Aaron's particular brand of bullshit.

"So what do you say, Asha, you going to invite me in?"

She blinked at him. Then cocked her head, trying to decide if he'd lost his damn mind or not. "That would be a no, Aaron. I'm having dinner with my brother soon, so I need to get ready."

His gaze narrowed. Whether he was pissed that she'd turned him down, or he was trying to decide if he believed her, it didn't matter. Either way, she gave zero fucks. Damn, Dax was a bad influence on her.

"I'm sure if I was Coulter, you'd find the time to spread wide for me, then."

Oh. Yeah, the little shit had lost his damn mind.

"Excuse me?" She took off her shoes so she could use them as weapons, should she need to.

"I know you think you're being slick. And you guys put on a good show. I mean, anyone looking wouldn't find a single instance of either of you acting inappropriately."

"He is my assignment. I don't know what you're talking about." Problem was, she'd always been a bad liar.

"See, the thing is, I'm good at reading people. It's the way you *don't* look at each other. The way you orbit each other but don't interact. Fuck, you smell like him half the time. Oh, and one night I was coming from an ice run and saw him leaving your room at 4:30 in the morning. Guy looked well used."

Her brain worked, trying to figure out when they'd ever been careless. There'd been one night a couple of weeks ago. *After we went to San Diego.* It had been in Miami, and they'd actually been working. Working naked, maybe, but they'd been going over the new endorsements that had come his way since the team started to win. He'd wanted her opinion. That, and video chat just hadn't cut it. They'd both needed to touch each other. "I don't know what you're talking about." All she wanted to do was get into the room. Even if Aaron was inclined to tell anyone, she and Dax would recover. It would be fine.

He sneered at her. "You act so fucking high and mighty. With all your 'I don't date' and 'I'm just here to work' bullshit. When what you really meant is, 'You don't have enough money to be worth my time.' He leaned in close, and the scotch on his breath had her recoiling. It didn't smell spicy and inviting like it did on Dax's breath.

"You've been drinking." They'd passed around a celebratory drink in the meeting, but it was looking like Aaron had had more than one.

"You don't even know the kind of guy you're fucking, unless you don't care." He grabbed her arm, and pain shot through her from her shoulder to pinky. She raised a shoe to go into full attack mode, but the next thing she knew, her arm was free and the scent of scotch no longer surrounded her.

She whipped around to find Damon and Dax in Aaron's face, fighting for the pleasure of ending his life. The flood of adrenaline made her head spin, and it took a second to realize Aaron was talking. And his face was bloody. Was that Damon or Dax? *Dax*. Blood dripped from his hand.

Aaron was saying something. "Does she know about the night at the club? The blonde. That you fucked her?"

What? Who did Dax fuck? Dax's brows snapped into a deep frown. "See that's the problem with lying. You'll always be found out. I never fucked some blonde at the club." The conviction in his voice made her heart soar.

Problem was Aaron was smirking. "Oh, really? Is that why I have a video of you getting a blowjob at Blink nightclub the night you met Asha there? From a woman appropriately named Barbie, of course. I was there. I saw you go off with the girl. I didn't think I'd get anything so good, but man, I found her again and hit paydirt. She'd been recording part of your tryst to show her boyfriend. I guess the joke's on you. Bitch is pregnant."

Asha's stomach roiled. Blonde from the club? What club?

Dax hadn't really been out much. He was on the phone with her every night. They were attached at the—no. No, they weren't. That first night she met with him. When she'd felt that spark. He'd stayed. *Oh, God.*

The look on his face told her everything. There had been a blonde. And just when she thought she was going to be sick, and the gray on the edges of her vision edged in, Damon let go of Aaron and his fist connected with Dax's face.

TWENTY-FOUR

"Dax, you're being stubborn for no good reason. Just call the lawyer."

Dax shook his head as he paced his living room. "No, Echo. I'm not doing it. This is not a Coulter problem. This is a Dax problem. I've worked really hard to distinguish myself from the fold, and I'm not running back because it's convenient."

His sister sighed. "Look, I understand. You want to stand on your own two feet. But if this girl goes to the press, or worse, that asshole leaks it, you're toast. All your hard work to become this new you is over."

He pinched the bridge of his nose. "Truth be told, I'm pretty sure no one expected this new me to last too long, right? What's the current bet on how long before I fucked up?"

His sister was silent for a beat too long. When she finally spoke, she said, "You are the only one who thought that. You. No one else, Dax."

"Oh, come on. You and I both know Gramps has money riding on me fucking up."

"That's enough. I love Gramps, but let's face it the geezer can be an asshole. Especially when it comes to you. Or, you know, something new. You've been locked in this battle for his approval for too long. You know, no one ever saw you as a screwup until you started playing to that. You have always been just as capable as the rest of us. But you thought it was your lot in life to take on the black-sheep mantle."

Shit, that burning, in his chest, it was back. The emptiness once again threatened to consume him. To take over. To engulf him and drag him down. "Echo, I liked being this me."

"Newsflash, twin brother. I like all the versions of you. Because they are part of you, and I always believed in you. You're the only one selling yourself short."

"Now you sound like Asha."

"Well, she's a smart girl."

He licked his lips and stopped in front of his fireplace, where a selfie of him and Asha had taken center stage amongst the family photos. Fuck, he missed her. "You never asked me if I slept with her."

Again his sister sighed. "Because it doesn't matter. Anything that happened, or didn't happen, would have been before you and Asha got together. Even if you couldn't see it, since she showed up you've been tuning to her frequency. One day, I hope someone looks at me how you look at her. That would be awesome. Besides, if you say you didn't sleep with her, I believe you. You have been an ass in the past, but you're no liar."

With her words, she peeled back another layer of fog he'd always assumed stood between him and his family. She knew him. Bryce saw him. He'd always held himself apart a little because he thought he needed to. But that was his own shit. "Thanks, Echo."

"Of course, what are—?" Her question was interrupted by movement into the room.

"Dax?"

He bit back the groan at the sound of his grandfather's voice on the line. The old man had commandeered the phone from his sister.

"I've been hearing rumblings, son. Did you pull a Dax again? Once again think with the little head instead of the big one? Because if you've jeopardized the Coulter—"

That was it. He had had it. "That's enough, Gramps."

There was a beat of silence then sputtering, and then his grandfather started again. "Now, you listen—"

"No, it's time for you to listen. You think I'm not good enough, you're entitled to your opinion. I, on the other hand, am no longer interested in hearing about it. Besides, thanks to winning, I get the rush of love from the fans now, so I don't need your approval anymore. And while I'm at it, I'm in love with Asha Wix. I know I might just about give you a coronary with that information. But I'm telling you that now so you have time to work your way around to that thought. No more off-color comments. No more mentions of her ethnicity unless it's to ask a thoughtful question."

"Now if you think—"

"Not done, Gramps. I love my name. I love how I grew up. But if the family can't let me be me, I will drop the last name and start going by Mom's maiden name or something."

"You wouldn't dare!"

"Watch me." And then Dax did something he'd never considered doing in his life. He hung up. No one in their right mind had ever told off Rory Coulter. Ever. First, he hoped Gramps survived. Second, he waited for the nervous anxiety, but it didn't come. He didn't need the old man's approval. Not anymore. Asha had changed that for him. He just hoped she took him back. Because he was going to go all-in with her. She was everything to him, and it was time he showed it.

Dax wiped his hands on his jeans, waiting for someone to answer. When the door whipped open, Damon cut an imposing figure. "D?" he nodded.

Damon just crossed his arms. "What do you want, Dax?"

"Dude, this whole thing is a fucking mess. I'm just trying to fix it. You're my best friend, and I need you to know I would never hurt her intentionally. That thing with that girl. I—that was *before* Asha. I didn't even...that girl is someone's sister, too, and well, I'm a dick. I've always been a dick. But for some reason the people in your family have faith in me, and I screwed that up."

Damon shook his head. "Shut up, Dax."

"No, man. I'm not shutting up. I came to talk to you, and I'm not leaving until it's said. I love Asha. And that girl, that happened when I was trying to do right by you and stay the fuck *away* from Asha. I was willing to take any out. Just as long as it wasn't Asha. Things with the two of us just spiraled so quickly and the next thing I know I'm falling for her hard. And that ache in my chest is almost unbearable. I would never have intentionally hurt her."

Damon shook his head. "You think I'm mad about some groupie? Shit, I've lost count of how many women I've slept with. I'm mad because you lied."

"No, Damon. I didn't. Yeah sure, I got a mediocre blowjob for my efforts, but I never slept with that girl. I don't lie to you. Not to the guy that's pulled my ass out of the fire a dozen times. And never to Asha."

Damon met his gaze and Dax held it, unwavering. It only took a minute, but then Damon's enormous shoulders sagged. "Shit. You really didn't sleep with her?"

"No, I really didn't. The tape Aaron claims to have is a fake. I didn't fuck that girl. She might be pregnant, but it's certainly not mine. You know me. This isn't my brand of asshole."

Damon nodded. "I know. I've known you almost half my life. You'll drink too much and sleep with a lot of women. Sometimes even at the same time. But you are unabashed at that. You keep the secrets, but you don't lie. I should have known it. It's just—this is my sister, man."

"I know. And it's killing me that I hurt her. That I hurt you."

"So what are you going to do?" Damon asked.

"Besides apologize to you? I haven't come up with much. I need to talk to her, but I haven't figured out how. I fucked this up."

"Well, you have to do the whole grand gesture thing. Off her feet and into your bed, or whatever. Make it a good gesture and she can't help but forgive you."

"I hope you're right about that."

TWENTY-FIVE

So this was what it meant to be lovesick. Well, Asha was tired of it. Frankly, it sucked. She'd take old, uptight Asha any day. At least that version of her didn't have a big, old, gaping hole where her heart used to be.

Every day, she woke up and put on her Asha suit. The one with the determined face that didn't cry at her desk or lick her wounds...on the outside. On the inside, she was a mess. Inside-her was walking around in her pajamas with ice-cream stains on them, and hadn't showered in three days. And had drunk-dialed and hung-up on Dax twenty-two times.

In truth, they hadn't spoken. Dax had walked away from her. He'd let Aaron go and looked between her and Damon. He hadn't said a word before he walked away. And afterward, no call, no nothing. Poof. Gone. Not a thing after the shit that went down a week ago. Her brother had taken her to the police to file a report.

Work passed in a blur. Aaron had been removed from his job. It turned out that Thrashers management really were zero tolerance. And she'd also learned that he'd made passes at two of the other girls on staff. He'd said he was going to sue Dax for hitting him, but she knew that was mostly bluster. Or at least she hoped so. The little shit would undo all her good work. *Not that you care anymore.* And of course, HR had been sincerely apologetic, wanting to know if she had other grievances to file. But all she wanted to do every day since that night was crawl into a hole and sleep. Either that or run to Dax's apartment and beg him to lie to her and tell her he didn't sleep with that girl.

With the team winning, babysitters were no longer needed, so she could focus more on traditional marketing. She found that more boring somehow. But with everyone gearing up for the playoffs, it was all-hands. She hadn't seen him in a week, and she missed him something awful. But she didn't have time to pout.

Sam was in town for a conference, and they had lunch plans. She would enjoy her time with her bestie and not sulk. She was in serious need of girl time.

When Sam showed up to meet her, it was pretty quiet at the office, as most everyone else had gone out for lunch. "So this is where the magic happens? Where you guys convince us a man with the nickname The Devil can also sell kids sports bottles or something?"

Asha laughed. "Something like that."

Sam sat back in Asha's seat and twirled, her thick, dark hair flying out as she did so. "If you don't mind me saying so, you look like hell. You fell in love, didn't you?"

"Sam, I just need you to hug me and tell me it's going to be okay right now, all right?"

"I would. Except you're not really one for hugs, and you've never wanted anyone to feed you any bullshit, so I'm going to kick it to you straight. You don't look good, babe."

"You think I don't know that? That I don't see the pitying looks people give me? Nobody here knew, but they suspected."

"Does he love you?"

Asha shook her head. "No."

"And you're sure of that? Because some girl said she slept with him?"

"You should have seen his face, Sam. And the way he just walked away from me."

Sam frowned. "All I'm saying is, maybe you should give the guy a chance to explain."

"I thought you said to stay away from him and not to be a *proho*."

"Well," Sam slid her gaze away. "That was before I saw how you looked. That picture of you two from the wedding. You looked so happy. I've never seen you that happy. And now you just look so sad. I want to fix it for you, and I think if you talked to him, you'd feel better."

"He's had all this time to talk to me. He hasn't even called." That was the shit that hurt the worst. She'd been waiting for him to call. To tell her something, anything. But nope. And besides sneaking to watch practice, she hadn't even seen him. It was like he was a figment of her imagination. "He would have called if he wanted me. And he hasn't."

Sam shrugged. "You ever think maybe he hasn't called because he thinks the one person that has had faith in him no longer does? That he is truly alone? Did that ever occur to you?"

Pain sliced through her chest. No. She'd never considered that. But he didn't even need her now. Hell, he hadn't really needed her before. He just needed some tweaking. *And he thinks you don't have faith in him.* And honestly, did she have faith? She kept thinking back to that look on his face. Horror and...something. Disbelief? Why the disbelief, though? Her gaze flickered to Sam's. "It never even occurred to me. I screwed up, huh?"

Sam shrugged. "Dunno. But maybe you should talk to him. Then maybe you'll stop looking like death warmed over. So lunch. But first, I want to see the field. My bestie works for a playoff team; I want a tour."

"Fair enough." How had everything gotten so messed up? *Things got messed up when you stopped trusting in him.*

She led Sam down to the hallway to the field. The main door was open, but it was eerily quiet. Usually, the place was teeming with people. When she walked out, Sam at her side, Dax walked toward them. Asha glared at Sam. "A setup?"

Her friend shrugged. "A conference, really? You believed that? Dude, the man loves you. He tracked me down. Flew me out here. Put him out of his misery."

The tears welled. *Oh, no. No, no, no.* She was not that girl who cried at work. But she wanted to be. Because when Dax walked toward her in jeans and a white T-shirt, he looked better than anything she'd ever seen in her life. And damn, she'd missed him.

WHAT IF SHE DOESN'T FORGIVE YOU? THE THOUGHT RAN through his head, over and over and over again. All week, he'd been trying to figure out what to say to her, who to be without her, and it all came back to the fact that he was better with her. Far better. And that empty feeling was gone. But not because of her, more because he let someone see him. And it felt good. He nodded at Sam. "Thank you for getting her here."

"Damn, you're pretty. I can see why she likes you."

Dax smiled briefly. "Thanks?" he phrased it like a question.

Sam laughed. "Any man who goes to all this trouble must be in love. You have my vote." She scampered off to join Damon and the others. "I'll call you when I get back to New Orleans, Ash."

"Dax, what did you do?" her voice was soft.

"I'm showing you I've been paying attention. Your whole life, you wanted people see you. Well, I see you, and yes, you're beautiful, but you're also smart, and funny, and kind, and patient. Fuck, are you patient. And you're tenacious and I am completely in love with you."

Her eyes went wide.

Shit. Now or never. He was going for broke. "And in case you need to hear it, I didn't sleep with that girl. Yes, we hooked up in the bathroom and frankly, it felt shitty, and I'm being honest when say I could barely keep it going. But the point is, I don't even know that girl. Yes, she blew me, but I didn't sleep with her. I spent the last couple of days sorting out lawyers and investigators to find her. For once, I handled things on my own. She's recanting her story. Aaron had tried to get her to leak the whole thing, but all she ever wanted was for her boyfriend to pay attention to her. And she wanted bragging rights. The whole thing just got completely out of hand."

"Dax."

"Let me finish, please. I know you thought I lied to you. But I didn't. I was so surprised when Aaron said she was pregnant. I was shell-shocked and confused, and I could see it on your face, and I thought you lost faith in me."

"Dax. I have had nothing but one hundred percent faith in you from the beginning. But you just walked away from me. Like I could be discarded in a heartbeat, and that hurt. That really hurt."

"I know, and I have been thinking of how to make that up to you in every way. I am in love with you. I have been ever since you walked into the training room and started bossing me around. I never should have walked away from you. I should have given you the chance to have faith in me. I am sorry. Please forgive me."

She rapidly blinked away tears, and he wasn't sure if that was a good thing. "Asha?"

"I love you, too."

Relief hit him square between the shoulders, and he wobbled. Oh, God. She was forgiving him. "I swear to God, I am never walking away from you again."

"I'm going to hold you to that."

TWENTY-SIX

Dax and Asha were the first ones to arrive at the Coulter estate for the family dinner. An impressive feat, given how long they had to drive to get there in the first place.

"Where's Echo?" Dax asked, as he and Asha were ushered into the sitting room for drinks. He'd been surprised at how easy it was to call his family back and let them know he was bringing Asha. Most of them had guessed that they were a couple after their disappearance from the wedding and hasty retreat the next morning. No one had said anything to the couple while they were together, but there had been plenty of questions for Dax in the days and weeks that followed. He'd told them all that they were still figuring things out. Until the press conference.

"Echo will be back soon," his dad told him from where he sat in his favorite chair by the fireplace.

"But we want to hear about the Pats game," Rory urged from his spot on the sofa next to Serina. "All that mess that happened. I want a play-by-play of those last few minutes. Those are the kinds of games you never forget," he said proudly.

"Uh... It was kind of a blur, actually," Dax recounted, as he accepted a drink from Asha, who perched next to him on the love seat. "I mean, obviously the plan was to head for the sideline—"

"Stop the clock," Rory interjected, with a nod of approval.

"But when I looked up and saw how open it was—except for that last guy—I just couldn't make myself do it." He looked to his father, who was smiling with pride and something else behind his eyes. But it was his grandfather's rapt attention that Dax found so interesting, and he turned back to the old man. "It was like I could see what was going to happen—just how and where he'd be when he got to me—and exactly what it would take to throw him off balance and get over him."

"If you can prove you have discipline and can follow instructions and go along with the order of things on the field and with your coaches, then in an instance like that where your gut instinct tells you something else and you go with it, they'll forgive you and respect you more after it—especially when it winds up winning the game," Rory said as he continued to nod.

It was unexpected. The complete and glowing approval from Gramps. Dax wasn't quite sure what to make of it, but the conversation was interrupted by his dad having a coughing fit over the green sludge in his cup.

Brent pulled out a handkerchief and waved off Julia, who looked ready to pat him on the back as though he were choking.

"I'm all right," he wheezed, as the coughing began to subside. "I just swallowed it wrong. Tickled my throat before it was all the way down."

"What the hell is that stuff anyway, Dad?" Dax asked. Whatever it was, it looked disgusting. "Please tell me it isn't some new protein drink thing that one of the suppliers wants you to put in the store."

His father shook his head as he wiped his mouth, though it was unclear whether the action was meant to refute Dax's speculation, or if it was simply from amusement over the comment.

"It's supposed to boost the immune system," Brent answered, his voice rough.

"Who needs a boost?" Echo asked as she and Gage walked in.

Gage had a duffel bag over his shoulder, and Dax watched as his brother glanced at their father, who motioned with a hand for him to go take care of his things. Gage gave a brief nod of acknowledgment to Dax and Asha, before ducking back out and heading for the stairs.

"Dad does, apparently," Dax answered Echo's question. "He nearly choked on that stuff in his glass. Can't be too good for your immune system if you choke to death on it."

"I'll keep that in mind," Brent wheezed. The redness in his face had faded, and he leaned back in his chair, sounding winded.

Echo sat next to Asha and the two began chatting, picking up a conversation they'd apparently begun at some other time, though Dax couldn't remember where or when. But before he could study on it much, he was distracted by Bryce and Tami's arrival.

"Sorry we're late, but we brought presents," Tami announced as Bryce helped hold the door.

"You're not supposed to *shop* on your honeymoon," Dax teased Bryce. "Or had you not heard what you *are* supposed to do?"

Tami rolled her eyes. Echo reached past Asha to give her twin a light punch to his biceps. Everyone else chortled or stifled their amusement, with varying degrees of success.

"For *that*, you don't get the Belgian chocolate we brought for you," Bryce muttered.

"Can *I* have it?" Asha asked.

"Sure," Bryce smiled, and Asha rose to go claim her prize,

quickly getting dragged into Tami's stories of the castles and museums they'd visited on their way across Europe.

"It was nice to actually *be* a tourist for a change. I'm still not used to traveling like that for tournaments, but when we're there to play, I hardly see anything except the hotel and the practice courts," she was explaining, holding up her phone to show Asha and Echo her pictures. Dax's mother and grandmother soon joined the crowd, and pressed Bryce for his opinions of the sites as well.

Gramps came and sat next to Dax.

"You did good in that game, son. I had my doubts about you, and I know I've been hard on you. But you have to understand... watching you play, knowing what you were capable of... I *knew* you had it in you. I just didn't think you would ever be able to... unlock it. Or maybe it was just that you didn't care to."

Dax swallowed to keep from snapping back. He was pretty sure Gramps meant to pay him a compliment, but the urge to tell him how bad he was at it was strong. He also knew better than to interrupt Gramps when he was *trying* to be nice. To do so was to risk it becoming an even more rare occurrence.

"It's amazing, isn't it, how meeting the right woman can make things...clearer?" Gramps said, with a nod to where Serina was pointing something out in the picture on the phone and answering Asha's questions. "She's a nice girl, your Asha. Don't screw it up." And with that, Gramps rose from his seat to go look at the honeymoon pictures himself.

It was only after he'd received such open praise from his grandfather that Dax could admit how desperately he'd been hoping to get it. And he realized that it wasn't just his grandfather who had been treating him differently lately. Though it was definitely more obvious with his family gathered together where he could see them face-to-face.

Their post-game calls had gotten lighter, and felt less like they were made out of habit or obligation, and more from genuine excitement. He didn't feel like they were trying to hide something from him when they addressed him. Their disappointment, their annoyance, their pity, even.

But was the change because of how he'd been playing or because of him? He felt more like himself lately, and less like he was putting on a show for someone, even if he wasn't always sure whom that someone was. Were they responding to that? He realized that while he appreciated their support and approval, it didn't thrill him the way he had always thought it would. He had spent so long pretending that he didn't care what his family thought about him or how he behaved, and yet he'd known all along that something had been missing.

Asha came over and plopped down beside him on the love seat. "The chocolate is *good*," she said, offering him a small piece. "Don't let it ruin your dinner," she warned.

He grinned at her, wrapping an arm around her shoulders to pull her in closer. "As if that could happen."

"You all right?" she asked, her brow furrowing.

He leaned in close to whisper, "They like you. Even Gramps."

She whispered back, "I know. They're starting to grow on me, too. I'm going to ignore the random insensitive shit."

He chuckled and kissed her temple, as the rest of the family party moved back into the center of the sitting room to take their seats and wait for Fox.

As they all settled in and listened to Bryce and Tami's honeymoon adventures, Dax wondered why having his family's approval didn't seem to mean as much to him anymore. Was it because he had it?

"I'm here," Fox called, as he strode through the main entryway. "Let's eat. I've got to head back out again as soon as we're done."

Echo rolled her eyes for everyone as she led the way to the dining room.

Dax and Asha had to take an early flight back to Florida so Dax could arrive in time to attend afternoon practice. Which he was determined not to miss, lest Coach Mills decide he needed to run laps for the rest of the season as retribution. Dax's parents insisted they stay at the mansion rather than pay for a hotel, arguing the desire to have breakfast together and see them off at the airport.

After dinner was over, Fox quickly disappeared, while Bryce and Tami, who had both been yawning all through dinner, decided to take off early in an effort to combat their jet lag. Gage had school in the morning and practice again in the afternoon, so he was sent upstairs to finish his homework. "I can't wait 'til the term ends," he declared, dragging himself away.

"We should turn in early, too," Dax said as he rose and held out a hand for Asha to take as she pulled herself up from her chair. "I need my forty winks, or I'll be knocked on my ass in practice tomorrow."

"Dinner was delicious," Asha told them as she set her napkin down and Dax tugged her toward the stairs. "And thank you again for having us stay."

"It's no trouble," she heard Julia say as they left the rest of the group behind with the dishes still on the table.

"I was going to offer to help—" She began to scold Dax when they reached the first landing, but he pressed her against the wall and kissed her before she could finish. "Mmm..." she murmured against his lips. "I think I'm gonna like what you have in mind better."

She let him lead her the rest of the way up the stairs and down the hall. Gage's open door was one of the first they passed. He looked up as they went by and reached for his headphones. Luckily Dax's room was at the far end of the hall.

Asha turned to lock the door behind them as Dax pressed his body against her back, the curve of her ass fitting nicely against his crotch. She drew a sudden breath as he wrapped his arms around her, curling her body to fit against his and running his hands down her torso to the waistband of her jeans.

"You really want to take me against the door when your little brother is studying down the hall?" she asked breathlessly.

"Fuck, yes," Dax whispered, nuzzling his nose against her neck and breathing her in. "I don't really care what they think."

As he said it, he understood how true it was. He didn't care what they thought anymore. He didn't need their approval because he had something he valued more—Asha. Well, he had what being with Asha gave him; faith in himself and his abilities, his own approval.

She sighed and pressed back against him, already bracing herself against the door.

His hands slipped below her waistband and she inhaled sharply.

"So are we officially public now? Media aside. We don't have to hide?" Dax asked, squeezing her ass before easing her jeans down her thighs.

Asha giggled. "I guess we are."

Dax trailed his lips down the back of her leg, his tongue darting out to tickle the sensitive flesh behind her knee. He felt the muscles in her leg tense as he left her jeans pooled at her ankles, and then he rose behind her, hands fumbling with his fly.

"What kinds of 'private things' are you suggesting we do in

public?" he asked suggestively before bending his head to kiss her shoulder.

She stopped his hand as it reached to see how ready she was for him. It was enough to hold him still while she slipped her feet from the legs of her jeans and panties so she could kick them lightly to the side. Still holding his hand, she turned around in the limited space between him and the door so that she faced him. The light fabric of her button-up shirt hung low, the hem skimming her bare thighs.

"Well for starters, holding hands," she said, glancing to where she held his wrist. "But if you think there's something *else* I could hold that might make our relationship a little clearer for everyone..." With her free hand she grasped his cock, making him gasp and step closer. He heard the slight tap of the door as she backed against it completely.

"I *do* think that would send a pretty clear message," Dax murmured before bending to kiss her again. She released his hand and his cock to slip her arms around his neck. He slid his arms around her and down her back, lifting her so she could wrap her legs around him as he slid into her, pressing her against the door and sliding into her slick depths, again, and again, and again. Being with her was like coming home. *Every. Damn. Time.*

EPILOGUE

Echo...
 Echo knocked on the bathroom door. "Cole, can we just talk?"
 "Jesus Christ, Echo, can't a guy get a little privacy?"
 She had zero idea what she was doing. Her IT band still throbbed some, but he'd helped her work out the kinks. At least those ones anyway. Right about now, she had other things on her mind. Other...*needs*. What just happened in the living room —it was the one thing that had felt like hers in weeks. It was also, unfortunately, the one thing she felt like she couldn't have.
 "Look, I'm sorry. Can we just talk about this? I don't even know what just happened. I just—could you just—"
 He dragged open the door. "What? What do you want from me, Echo? I don't want to play this game anymore. I'm your coach. That's it. I don't need you just dicking with me."
 "I'm not. I swear, I just have zero experience with this, and I don't know what to do."
 He dropped his hand and stalked back into the bathroom. "Are you fucking serious right now? Look, Jen said that maybe that first night that wasn't your plan. But the other night, at

Living Green, you meant to do that. That kiss you gave me, you were dicking with me. And here's the worst thing. I knew you didn't mean it, but that still didn't stop me from wanting you. All night. Hell, all weekend, it's all I could think about. How you fucking taste, the way you move, the way your muscles clamped around my thighs."

Her breath caught as her gaze flickered over his body, eventually landing on the bulge in his jeans. *Wow.*

Need pulled low in her belly. She wanted him. She'd always wanted him. *The two of you are a bad idea.* She loved how she felt with him. *He doesn't want to want you.* She wanted to be the strong, confident woman she was the night they met. *You will regret this.* For once in her life she didn't care.

With a deliberate step forward, she pushed into the bathroom and locked the door behind her. "You want me to help you with that?"

His entire body shook on his exhale. When he spoke, he voice was rough, but pleading. "Echo, you keep looking at me like that, we're going to do something about what you're staring at."

"Good, we're on the same page."

His brows snapped down. "Don't play with me. I'm not—"

Taking another bold step, she pressed her fingertips to his mouth. "You talk too much."

Cole's eyes darkened, even as his gaze narrowed and a shiver ran through her. "What do you want from me, Echo?"

Smoothing her hand over his rock-hard abs, she whispered, "I want to feel something other than worry or exhaustion for five minutes. I want to feel something that's mine." She reached for his buckle. He groaned low and squeezed his eyes shut.

"Shit, Echo."

She hesitated, the uncertainty washing over her. He didn't

want her, after all? She pulled her hand back. "Do you want me to stop?"

His dark gaze bore into hers. "Fuck no." Reaching for her, he slid his hands into her hair, clamping his hand on the back of her neck. The kiss he gave her wasn't teasing, it wasn't a question. It was a statement about possession. His tongue slid into her mouth, and heat bloomed in her core, making her desperate.

She tugged on his zipper, the sound mingling with their moans. But when she reached into his boxers, Cole dragged his lips from hers and hissed in a breath.

"Sorry. Did I—"

Again, she tried to pull away, but he held her still. "Stay." His guttural command was like a mating call to her libido, and something bloomed inside her. Like the other night, but this time she wasn't pretending. This time, it was all her, and she was driving him crazy, just with her touch.

She wrapped her fingers around the length of him and his body shook. Cole went back to kissing her as she tentatively stroked him. His hips bucked and his tongue mimicked the thrusting of his dick in her hands. Matching time and tempo.

She pulled him free of his boxers, and marveled at how soft the skin covering his smooth tip was.

When she used her thumb to gently rub in the bead of moisture over the tip, his knees buckled, and he took a small step to steady himself. "Oh God. Echo." He moaned into her mouth. He tried to hook his thumbs into her workout shorts to tug them down, but she pulled back. She wanted to drive. And if he made love to her, there was no way she was going to be in charge of anything. She'd happily turn her body over to him and melt into a puddle of lust.

"I want to be in charge, Cole."

His gaze met hers, and he seemed to understand. Nodding

slowly, he said, "It's your show, Echo. I want you any way I can get you."

She licked her lips. "Okay." She stroked him down to the root again, then back to the tip, smoothing her hand over all of him. Did he like this? Was she any good? Even as her confidence grew, there was something about the harsh light of day to shake some of her newfound moxie. "Can you— Can you help me? I want to know what you like. That I'm doing it right."

Cole drew in a shuddering breath. "Your hand is on my dick. That's pretty much a great start right there." But still he laid his larger hand over hers, tightening her grip and upping her tempo.

She watched his face intently as they stroked him together. His eyes were on their now-intertwined hands as they worked him, and sweat beaded on his brow. And every time they reached the tip and she stroked her thumb over the underside of him, his eyes rolled into the back of his head.

Note to self, touch here again. And do it often. It wasn't long before she added the rubbing of her hand over the crown of him on every up stroke. He eventually let go of her hand and used that hand to grip the edge of the counter, even as he gently, but firmly, tugged on her hair.

Hushed curses and the constant chanting of her name was all she could hear as her brain drowned out anything that was not happening inside this locked bathroom. Nothing was going to intrude. She needed this time for herself with Cole. This time where she could be wanted and desired simply because she was herself.

"Yes, fuck, Echo. God, it's like you were made for me." His hips rocked into her hand, his voice going guttural and his tempo increasing. "So close. Fuck, fuck, fuck. I'm going to come." His eyes squeezed shut as his release bore down on him.

"Please look at me, Cole." If they were only going to get this stolen moment, she wanted to feel some of that initial connection. Wanted to know it was her he wanted. She wanted to feel it.

His eyes snapped open, and the heat of his gaze burned through her. His body went tight, and if possible, the already thick length of him expanded in her hand. With a low, feral growl, he pulled her in for a kiss, even as his release broke, and his warm seed poured over her hand.

His kiss was equal parts tender and desperate, as if he was just as eager to hold on to this moment as she was. Echo kissed him back with every ounce of need and passion and desperation she had in her body. To her surprise, instead of going soft, his dick hardened again.

He moaned into her mouth, then whispered, "Did you like being in control?"

Even as she dragged in ragged breaths, she nodded. "Y-yes."

"Good. My turn now."

His? *Oh. Ohhhh.* He lifted her easily to sit on the counter. He pulled one of the washcloths from the shelf, and quickly cleaned all traces off himself from her hand and hip. Then he tossed the washcloth on the counter before stepping between her thighs. "I've been fucking dreaming about this again since that morning you walked out."

Before she could argue that she hadn't meant to leave him, distant sounds of someone calling her name had them both freezing. Well, except for his cock. His erection continued to bob happily between them. Teasing her center with promises of fun to come.

Cole swore under his breath, even as she whimpered. Her parents were home. Hell.

Cole was surprisingly calm as he righted his clothes. "Go, take a shower. I'll see you down here for the sit down with the family."

She stared at him for a second, unable to do anything but blink. He thought she could just pretend that everything was normal? "I—Cole?"

He tucked himself back into his jeans and kissed her deep. "We'll talk about this later." He shrugged. "Right now, we have a meeting and we both need to keep it together."

Damn it, the meeting. She'd totally forgotten the whole reason for them working on the estate today. She hopped off the counter and tossed the washcloth onto the hidden hamper. "Oh, my God." Had she really just done that?

Cole pulled her close, but he didn't kiss her again. "It's fine. We'll talk later."

Emotions roiling inside of her, she nodded and unlocked the door. When she let herself out, she didn't look back.

Do not stare at Echo.

It was a simple command. One his lust-fogged brain could barely send to his eyes. Given the effort put into the command, he would think his eyes would be more inclined to pay attention.

Yeah, not easy. Try as he might, he couldn't help but steal covert glances at her. And given the occasional spike of prickly heat he'd feel every few minutes or so, she was looking at him, too.

He had no idea what the fuck had just happened, but he wanted it to happen again. Right the fuck now. He didn't know exactly what was up with her, but there was something going on. Something besides the training. Whatever it was, it had to be the reason for the bags under her beautiful eyes, and her distraction. She'd needed him, and if he was being honest, he'd needed her too. He'd been fighting the attraction for so long, hiding behind his anger, but like it or not, the two of them were combustible.

But not just that, there was a vulnerability about her that pulled at him. He wanted to ease what was worrying her. He wanted to make it better. He wanted to protect her. *Because you're a fool.* Maybe he was, but he was willing to admit he'd been wrong about her. Maybe a little.

He looked up to find Brent Coulter looking at him expectantly. Shit. What were they talking about? "Sorry. My mind was somewhere else. What was that?"

Rory harrumphed. "And this is the man we have training her? He can't keep his focus."

Cole didn't bother rising to the bait. "I'm going over every eventuality for what might happen at the race. Sorry."

Brent shook his head. "No, of course. I was just checking to see if you wanted any changes made to the reservation; do you have any family you want us to add a hotel room for?"

Oh, that. Alex would love to come, but Cole wasn't going to do that. He didn't want to be beholden to them in any way. "No. Just me."

Rory muttered from the corner. "I guess the Biltmore is a step up from where you'd normally stay."

Cole didn't need to rise to the occasion. Echo beat him to it. "Gramps, enough. I have enough to think about without you harping on my coach."

Cole didn't dare look at her. Everything he was thinking and feeling would be written on his face for everyone to see. Instead, he looked at the old man, who stared at his granddaughter.

Looked like Echo was coming into her own, and damn if that didn't make him want her more.

You are a Coulter. You will be perfect. That's what Echo has been told every day of her life. As

the only girl in the Coulter clan, she knows it's her job to be the glue of the family. But with the Olympics looming, the last thing she wants is to follow the rules. She wants to break free, and she knows just the guy to help her. Meet Echo in book 3 of the Player Series

THANK YOU

Thank you for reading DAX! I hope you enjoyed the second book in my new series, The Player.

Would you like to know when my next book is available? You can sign up for my new release newsletter here, visit me at www.nanamalone.com, follow me on twitter at @NanaMalone, or like my Facebook page at www.facebook.com/nanamalonewriter. And if you want to chat with other peeps who love my books and spread the word, you can join my Sassy Street Team here!

Reviews help other readers find books. I appreciate all reviews. Please leave a review on your retailer's site or on Goodreads to help other readers discover the Series.

Don't miss any of the next Player books!

Bryce

Dax

Echo

Fox

Ransom

Gage

NANA MALONE READING LIST

Looking for a few Good Books? Look no Further

FREE
Sexy in Stilettos
Game Set Match
Shameless
Before Sin
Cheeky Royal

Royals
Royals Undercover

Cheeky Royal
Cheeky King

Royals Undone
Royal Bastard
Bastard Prince

Royals United
Royal Tease
Teasing the Princess

Royal Elite

The Heiress Duet
Protecting the Heiress
Tempting the Heiress

The Prince Duet
Return of the Prince
To Love a Prince

The Bodyguard Duet
Billionaire to the Bodyguard
The Billionaire's Secret

London Royals

London Royal Duet
London Royal
London Soul

Playboy Royal Duet
Royal Playboy
Playboy's Heart

The Donovans Series
Come Home Again (Nate & Delilah)
Love Reality (Ryan & Mia)
Race For Love (Derek & Kisima)

Love in Plain Sight (Dylan and Serafina)
Eye of the Beholder – (Logan & Jezzie)
Love Struck (Zephyr & Malia)

London Billionaires Standalones
Mr. Trouble (Jarred & Kinsley)
Mr. Big (Zach & Emma)
Mr. Dirty (Nathan & Sophie)

The Shameless World

Shameless
Shameless
Shameful
Unashamed

Force
Enforce

Deep
Deeper

Before Sin
Sin
Sinful

Brazen
Still Brazen

The Player
Bryce
Dax

Echo

Fox

Ransom

Gage

The In Stilettos Series
Sexy in Stilettos (Alec & Jaya)

Sultry in Stilettos (Beckett & Ricca)

Sassy in Stilettos (Caleb & Micha)

Strollers & Stilettos (Alec & Jaya & Alexa)

Seductive in Stilettos (Shane & Tristia)

Stunning in Stilettos (Bryan & Kyra)

~~~

In Stilettos Spin off
Tempting in Stilettos (Serena & Tyson)

Teasing in Stilettos (Cara & Tate)

Tantalizing in Stilettos (Jaggar & Griffin)

Love Match Series
*Game Set Match (Jason & Izzy)

Mismatch (Eli & Jessica)

Don't want to miss a single release? Click here!

ABOUT NANA MALONE

USA Today Bestselling Author, Nana Malone's love of all things romance and adventure started with a tattered romantic suspense she borrowed from her cousin on a sultry summer afternoon in Ghana at a precocious thirteen. She's been in love with kick butt heroines ever since.

Nana is the author of multiple series. And the books in her series have been on multiple Amazon Kindle and Barnes & Noble bestseller lists as well as the iTunes Breakout Books list and most notably the USA Today Bestseller list.

Want to get notified of Nana's next book? Text SASSY to 313131!

Made in United States
Troutdale, OR
11/27/2023